THE FOREST
PATH

THE FOREST PATH

Six Tales of Enchantment based on Wildflower Folklore

Meg Grimm

Story Spinner Press

Published by
Story Spinner Press
Ohiopyle, Pennsylvania
www.storyspinnerbooks.com

For information about permission to reproduce selections from this book,
write to thepost@storyspinnerbooks.com.

First Printing, December 2020

Printed in the United States of America

ISBN 978-1-7347867-6-7

Library of Congress Control Number: 2020925696

PREFACE

What you hold in your hands are the stories that marked the beginning of my journey as a writer. Most of these tales are my earliest complete writings. I began to pen them one day having told myself that if I was ever to learn how to write, I needed to *write*. That was, after all, what every book about writing really said. (Now you don't have to buy any yourself.)

For a long time, these stories were my practice. I wanted to find out if I could write outside of what I knew. Could I write from a man's perspective? From a child's? Could I write in the third person as well the first? Could I write an action scene just as well as a love story? Could I write about a lifestyle, a time period, or a region I knew not of? Could I describe the behavior of wolves? Or blackened battlefields? Could I create magic and make someone fall in love?

At the time, I was already being drawn to folklore, but I didn't know it. I thought my obsession with wildflower lore was an interest in herbs and plants. The two came together to became a thread connecting all these very different stories. And as it turned out, that thread would set the stage for my writing to come.

I never thought I would publish these so-called practice stories, but they have became a significant part of me. I have revisited them innumerable times through the years.

I recall the first time someone with credentials said that people would like reading them. Over time, others who I thought should know said so, too.

That's not why I finally decided to publish *The Forest Path*. When I was told that someone might like to read these stories, it was at that time that I first began to call myself a *writer*. Before that, I felt it was a sacred honor that could only be bestowed upon me by a publishing house. I could not simply claim it.

But I decided then that if I was going to be a writer, I must own my craft. Whether I was a good or bad writer was yet to be known, and there would be room for improvement all my life. But I was a writer just as much as any other. And one day, I would be a published author if I kept doing what writers did.

Whether or not you do like reading these stories as some thought you might, I thank you for giving them, and me, a chance. They represent the beginning of a wonderful adventure. I hope you might stick with me on it. The beginning is always a bit bumpy, but the summit is worth the climb.

I've always wondered where the forest path will go.

Meg Grimm

December 2020

CONTENTS

CONTENTS

RED MEANS LOVE

In Roman mythology, roses represent pain, suffering and death.
Today, tradition has attached associations to rose color.
Red means love.

THERE WAS SO much Joshua wanted to tell Addie. Like that right now he was perched in the opening of a Black Hawk prepared to dive out into the hazy, war-smoked sky before him. Even if he could, would she understand any better now than she had before? Although a life needed saved in the combat zone below, somebody else could do it, she would say.

A droplet of sweat trickled into his eye. He blinked and shook his head. He rarely thought of Addie at a time like this when a mission was moments away. She was part of his other life, the one separated from the world of the military. So why was her face in his mind now staring at him with those deliberate eyes? I told you so, she seemed to say.

Something was wrong. But it couldn't be. He had done this so many times before. Through the dust and debris he could make out the contours of the dry, tawny earth below. It looked just like the maps. He could visualize the mission with sureness of every step. Simple. Uncomplicated. No different than any other mission in other deployments. So, why the uneasiness in the pit of his stomach? It was growing. That was unmistakable. And why was he thinking of Addie?

"Ready!" It was an order rather than a question from the aircraft pilot. In the corner of his eye, Joshua caught a glimpse the man's red face. Instantly, another red face flashed into his thoughts. He saw the bully, Johnny Olson, from his days at Oaksdale Elementary sauntering across the pavement of the playground. Joshua sat cross-legged with a basketball in his lap. Suddenly, he was eye level with Johnny's scarred, knobby knees.

"Joshua loves Addie!" Johnny sneered, an evil jack-o-lantern grin revealing two chipped teeth carved into his round face.

"No, I don't!"

"You gave her a red flower. I saw it! Red means love. Joshua Perry loves Addie Huckabie!"

Joshua shook the visions away. This was not the time. He refocused his gaze on the earth.

He was ready, wasn't he? He was always ready.

The blades of the Black Hawk thundered overhead. Joshua took a deep breath and allowed the sound to drown out all other noise and become a beating drum in his soul. It was the sound of mission. It was the sound of destiny. It was the sound that pushed him forward. In less than a minute he would be rappelling through the open air. This would begin and would not end until the mission was complete. It would not end as planned unless they all did everything precisely. He could rely on the other soldiers posted next to him. No one ever wavered on a mission.

The Black Hawk jerked slightly and a gust of damp wind smacked him.

The wind carries your message.

Another face rushed into his mind, this one from the depths of his memories. It was a face he knew well, but it was the face of long ago. The big, bright eyes of a little girl bore into his.

The wind carries your message, Addie had said when they were just children. She had long hair then.

He shook his head. What was going on?

Joshua assumed the position to jump, his body rigid and jaw set. His eyes blazed down at the war-torn land. The Black Hawk lowered. In an instant that seemed to stand timeless, as instants like this one always did, the command was given. Joshua and his comrades fell into the air.

All at once her face appeared again. The lure of her eyes pulled him into their gaze with sudden control as no other force could, not even the need to focus on his descent. He peered into their gray-green. Wind whipped his body as though he were caught in a swirling tornado. A dark cyclone of dread. Why was this happening? His intuition finally began to take over, but it was too late.

Her lips parted.

The wind carries your message to the one you love. Grandma told me, so I know it's true. … Love does it. Love does magic things. … Joshua? Where are you going? Will you come back? Come back soon, Joshua… Promise you'll come back...

The phantasm vanished, and Joshua barely had time to prepare for landing. No sooner had his feet touched the Iraqi soil than the shooting began. Darting for cover behind some small fortified hills, he heard shouting. The enemy moved in, but the side gunners of the orbiting aircraft were covering him.

Dodging debris and staying low to the ground, Joshua moved almost supernaturally, zigzagging in and out of danger like lightning. He was the fastest. He was the best.

"That's why you're here," Commander Houck had told him when he arrived at camp.

Joshua bounded over a ditch, dropped and rolled through an exposed notch in the hills. He was on his feet again in seconds. As expected, a crumpled body came into view only fifteen feet away.

Private Lowery lay motionless on the ground hardly protected from the enemy's fire. In a swift, powerful motion, Joshua was beside him covering the man's body with his own and pulling him away from the crest of a hill. Bullets whizzed through the air and ricocheted off the earth around them. The Private's eyes were closed. A diamond shaped piece of shrapnel protruded from his torso. Thick blood seeped from the wound. Not bright red as blood from a surface cut, but the red gore from inside. There was not much time.

"Hang in there!"

He carefully pulled the private down the bank until they were protected by the hill. Then he heaved him up and ran. The muscles in his legs enflamed with power and adrenaline. Just as he reached the evacuation point, he spotted some of the squad. Together they would transport Lowery to a safe location on the other side of a nearby Iraqi village. This was almost over.

Just then, a blast erupted directly in front of them. Rocket propelled grenades. The whole world seemed to quake as black smoke filled the air. Joshua dropped Lowery to the ground and hunched over him. He could hear debris falling all around as particles showered them.

The once nearing sound of heavy Black Hawk blades retreated. They would be back. They were prepared for the unexpected. Under him, Lowery lay motionless. But he was not gone. Not yet.

"Lowery! Stay with-"

Another explosion burst toward them. A piece of charred metal whirled through the smoke and collided with Joshua's helmet. Another larger piece struck his right ankle, crushing it.

He was stunned for a moment. Then the pain seared through him belatedly. That was always the way. Addie's voice pierced through the noise.

Joshua!

Focus.

The sound of war blared everywhere, but the sound of the Black Hawk had vanished. They would not have pulled off farther than three hundred feet. He should still hear them. If they did not swing around soon, then there was no cover.

All at once, he realized what was happening. It was too dangerous. In the meantime, the squad would have to hold up in a defensible location. Where were the others? This wasn't right. He reached for his radio system.

Command sounded garbled and distant. Find cover. Remain. They would send help. Where were the others? There were no others.

Joshua shook off the shocking news and looked down at the private. The mission. Unsnapping his first aid kit, he clenched his teeth as he endured the raw sting of his own wounds.

"They're dying!"

"Of course, they're dying. Flowers don't last forever. You have to stop sulking or you'll make yourself sick."

Addie picked up her head from the kitchen table and made a face at her friend. A glass vase of wild red roses sat between them. The gray water had developed a light film, and the petals drooped.

"I don't know what to do with myself, Jules. This is worse than I thought."

"I could make a suggestion," Julie said, winking.

"Ohh," Addie moaned. "I know I should start working again, but I just don't have the energy."

"How much energy does it take to pick up a paint brush?"

"It's not that. I can't paint like *this*. Without him in the states, I'm too anxious."

Julie shook her head. She began to clear the table of their breakfast dishes. "I know it's scary, Adoline, but Joshua is strong. We just have to trust God. If you don't put your chin up, you'll be a mess by the time he comes home. And he will be coming home."

Addie put her head back down and listened to the sounds of her roommate tidying the kitchen.

"All right," Julie said. "I'm leaving. I really think you should work on a painting. Get back into a routine. Don't just lay around, got it?"

Addie made a small sound of defeat. "Jules, why didn't he ask me to marry him?" She looked up in time to see her friend search for words.

"He only went overseas, Adoline. You don't have to question if he loves you. I see a big bunch of roses that show it."

Red means love.

Addie remembered Joshua told her that once, ages ago, when he was the little boy from next door who came to play in her backyard. He never minded telling her exactly what was on his mind then. That had changed. Did he love her now? Enough to marry her? She thought so, but he had never said it. A man of few words. That was Joshua now.

Addie gazed at the roses. She felt Julie kiss the top of her head and leave, closing the door behind her.

The kitchen had been filled with the sweet aroma of the roses when Joshua first brought them. He had cut them from the rose bush at his mother's house. Her favorite. It was easier to pretend he was not far away when the roses remained lovely and thriving, but each day they wilted more. She dreaded the day when they would be dead, completely dead.

Addie remembered when Joshua had told her he was enlisting in the army. His parents were proud, especially his military father. Joshua came from a long line of military men. His grandfather and great grandfather had been in the navy. Joshua showed her their photographs. They were hanging in his bedroom. She should have known.

His haircut was the first big shock. Joshua always had a full head of ebony curls. Seeing his shaven scalp only proved he was moving on to do a job that would change their lives forever.

"Everyone is happy for me except for you," he'd accused her.

It was different seeing photographs of men who had fought in the older wars. The ones that were long over. To imagine Joshua in danger overseas was overwhelming. She was proud of him, sure. But she wanted to spend her life with him, not mourn his death before he had even asked her to marry him. The news channels flashed endless images of blood, smoke and desert. Statistics climbed. The War on Terror showed no sign of an end. Did Joshua have to charge headfirst into that?

Joshua's fate wasn't the only thing that worried her. She had noticed small changes, too. Secrets. He would be working apart from the danger of the battlefield, he had said. He was an engineer. She had no reason to worry so much. Except what was that in his eyes? The familiar glint was overcast. There were shadows between the two of them now. Things he didn't tell her. He couldn't tell her, he said.

Don't worry. Don't worry. He repeated it over and over.

She remembered how he had looked when he gave her the roses. Subdued. Did he feel the same apprehension she did? That it could be the last time they would ever see eachother? Joshua was the only man she had ever loved. She had loved him from the time she was a little girl.

She shook herself trying to rid the thoughts. Julie wanted her to paint today. Maybe she would.

Addie had been surprisingly successful with her art so far. She had a suitable studio in one of the upstairs rooms, and she taught five students. She was always able to keep herself in materials at least. Painting took passion though. She had tried to explain that to Julie many times. It would be difficult to create a piece while feeling this way. Then again, at this point, she was willing to do whatever it took to get her mind off Joshua's possible peril.

"I'll give it a go," she whispered aloud, willing herself to commit.

The art studio was a small room with one window overlooking the street below. It was the one place in the house where she did not have to be neat and organized. Unfinished paintings propped against the walls and color splattered upon the tile floor and the counters. Rows upon rows of tube paints made a rainbow across a shelf the length of the wall.

Addie secured a new canvas on her easel. She stared at its emptiness and sighed. She had no inspiration. Not a single spark of an idea. Taking a deep breath, all she could smell was old paint and thinner. Not the lovely scent of roses. They were downstairs fading away. Like her dreams.

All her hopes for a quiet, uncomplicated life with Joshua seemed to be disappearing into the past where her childhood lived. She had concocted these dreams then when she twirled around in pink princess costumes and made wishes on shooting stars. If she could only find a way to stop time, to make the good in life last before it slipped through her fingers. To make her roses, a symbol of Joshua's love given to her, live on forever.

She absently scanned the tubes of paint until her eyes rested on the color of her hope.

Red means love.

It would not be as good as having the real thing, but at least in this small way she could keep the roses.

Joshua had been in his uniform on his way out when he gave them to her. She gathered them from his hands like they were made of glass. "They're perfect," she said. Her hands were shaking. Joshua stood quietly in her kitchen doorway watching her as she fumbled in the cabinets for a vase.

"You're perfect," he said softly.

Addie squirted a small dot of red paint onto her palette. She dipped the tip of a brush into thinner while blinking away tears. A single drop slid down her cheek and into the paint.

"Please God, keep him safe. Please let him be okay and feel my love, no matter what he faces," she prayed aloud.

A great calm washed over her. "I love you, Joshua," she murmured and began to hum. Humming was an old habit that she did when she painted. It was reminiscent of her grandmother. The old woman would rock in her rocking chair as she knit and sang.

I've knit with love today, Grandmother would say. *Do you know how powerful love is, Addie? It's stronger than anything else on earth. It can do things you never would imagine. Magical things.*

Addie hummed for hours as she painted, moving the brush slowly at first and then becoming absorbed in her work. The yellow sun filled the room during the day. In the late afternoon sky, it hung as a tired, orange orb.

Finally, when Addie was nearly finished, she absently wiped

the last wet, love-soaked tears from her cheeks and reached out with the same fingertips to smudge a bit of paint in the center of one of the roses. The tears touched the canvas and dried as though melting into the painting.

She had to admit the roses looked pretty. She'd painted them with much more life than the real ones sustained now. She had darkened their stems and enriched the petals. They were tied together with a cherry red ribbon instead of cramped in the glass vase.

After adding a finishing touch to a pointed leaf and then a brush of brown to the tip of a shadow, she dropped her brushes into thinner. The painting was finished. Her roses would live on. So would Joshua. He would come home to her. He had to.

Addie stretched the muscles in her back and put away her paints. She may not feel better about Joshua being deployed somewhere far from her, but at least she had done something productive today. That did give her a sense of normalcy after all, she decided. She was grateful for Julie. She looked at the piece once more and blinked the last tears from her eyes.

Downstairs, Addie scrubbed the paint from her hands with a soapy sponge. Red water churned in the sink below. She watched it uneasily. Wiping her hands, she reddened a dish cloth. She shuddered, quickly burying it in bundle of dirty laundry.

Outside, the sun dropped below the horizon. Julie would be home any minute. It was time for dinner. Addie lifted a pot to the sink and began to fill it with water.

As if on cue, her roommate emerged into the kitchen.

"I'm home!"

"Hi, Jules."

"You're making dinner? Thank goodness, I'm starving!"

Addie hesitated. "I... made something else, too."

"Stop! You don't mean a painting, do you?"

Addie smiled slightly.

"Oh, honey, that's great! Show me!"

Julie threw her purse and keys on the table. The two friends scampered upstairs and into the studio.

"I couldn't think of what to paint," said Addie breathlessly. "Then it just came to me. I was so upset about the roses dying. I just love him so much, and I wished I could hold onto them until he comes back."

"So, where's the painting?"

"What do you mean?"

Addie turned to the easel where she'd left the painting of the roses, but to her surprise, the canvas was blank.

Joshua lay on his back. The sky was still filled with smoke and dark clouds, but the sounds of war had died down. Beside him, Private Lowery was breathing choppily as he slept, dust clogging his throat. Joshua had dressed both of their wounds, but he was faint with exhaustion himself.

He closed his eyes. Addie. What if they didn't come back for them in time? What if he lost his life right here in this desert far from home? What if he was never going to see her again? It couldn't end like this. Would she ever forgive him? He would never keep anything from her again. No matter how she felt about his real job. If God would give him a second chance, Addie would know he planned to ask her to marry him just as soon as he could buy the ring.

With fear ebbing into his heart, he strained to feel Addie's love even in a place so far away. He squeezed his eyes shut tighter, picturing her face.

She smiled down at him as lovely as ever. Then her lips began moving. She was whispering. What was she saying? He couldn't understand. There were only the soft wisps of words melting into the breeze and falling down around him. Then one fell on his cheek.

He opened his eyes and grabbed the paper-thin object. It felt smooth like velvet between his fingers. Then he heard the soft landing of another one beside his ear. What were these?

Peering deep into the sky, he saw them floating down. Small, circular pieces of something dark and feathery. They seemed to swirl through the smoke and rest only around him.

He grasped a handful of them as they fell and caught a sweet scent mingling in the thick air. Could these be...? Rose petals?

Then the wind carried on it a familiar whisper. Was he dreaming? Dying? Feeling meek and silly, he said, barely audibly, "Addie?"

"I love you, Joshua," the frail voice of the wind breathed. It began to hum. It was her. It had to be.

The wind carries your message. Love does it. Love does magic things.

Joshua closed his eyes in wonder as he focused on the sound. All the while, rose petals of the deepest red tumbled gracefully from the sky and fell upon him.

When they ceased, a single, bright red ribbon followed them down, twirling like a dream. It curled itself across his sooty hand, which rested upon his heart.

He thought he was mistaken for a moment, but soon he was very sure he heard the sound of Black Hawk blades heading toward them from the distance.

THE CHURCHYARD

Wood betony was once planted in churchyards or worn as an amulet to drive away evil spirits. It was said that if a serpent was caught in a bed of betony, it would lash itself to death.

A WIND LIKE THE rush of a thousand whispers charged through trees toward Kyler. He opened his eyes. The moon peered from behind a thick cloud far above illuminating the lonely field. It was going to storm.

Kyler lay on his back staring up the long stems of bulbous yellow flowers and high grasses. The vibrant petals poked the dark sky and seemed to press down on him hard and deep. He tried to move, but his body felt made of stone. Dead almost.

"You got a safe place to put this?" Old Man Southern's voice came from somewhere nearby.

"My wallet's as safe a place as any," Kyler heard himself say.

Even though he couldn't see the old man, he could feel his disapproving gaze. It made his stomach lurch.

"I woulda metcha et the bank, son," the voice said.

"Eh, it's alright. It just has to wait till morning. Thanks again. You saved my life."

"Happy to help ya out anyways I can." Then fading away, "Never been much for superstition myself."

"What?"

Suddenly, the powerful wind burst across the field with a loud howl that sounded like…like…

Murphy?

It's a dream, he realized.

Kyler stirred unwillingly from sleep and opened his eyes for real. No field. No moon. No sleeping straight through the night even though he had to be up at 5am.

The muffled howls and barks of the dog in the kennel outside melted into crisp, irritating noise.

He instinctively groped for his wallet on the nightstand and gave the stuffed leather a protective squeeze. No one knew. No one knew he had ten grand all wadded up in his measly wallet. They couldn't. He was still broke for all anybody knew. Had been for months.

What time was it? He squinted at the red numbers of his alarm clock.

2:23.

What was Murphy barking about? A stray cat, probably. Or maybe headlights down the road. He should have just let the dog spend the night inside so Murphy wouldn't hear every cricket and alert the whole neighborhood.

Cha-Chink.

Kyler froze. That was sound of the front door handle.

Locked. He had locked up before he went to bed, he remembered. Maybe Murphy had a reason to bark after all.

Kyler sat up in the stillness straining his ears and hoping for a familiar knock. He wasn't accustomed to visitors at this hour, but it wouldn't be altogether out of place. Many of his buddies were out of work lately. Half of the beach was out of work.

Nothing.

He eased out of bed and found the crumbled jeans from the floor where he had left them. He tugged them on, and his boots. Every muscle in his body ached, but he hardly noticed. A long, hard day's work had put food in his belly and gave him a sense of security that had been missing for months.

He slipped his knife from his pocket and crept down the stairs. Standing back from the front door at the bottom, he cautiously peered through the window into the yard. It was darker outside than usual. Maybe tomorrow's rain was here already.

Murphy's eyes glistened from across the yard. Nothing appeared out of the ordinary.

Kyler put his hand on a switch, hesitated, and then flicked on the porch light. The dog's ears perked up.

"Ok, buddy. You've gotta come in so I can get some sleep," Kyler muttered, opening the door. No one would try to come into a house with a Rottweiler anyway. He examined the shadows of the yard one last time and darted to the kennel.

"Get in the house," he commanded, unlatching the gate.

The dog bounded for the porch and leapt onto it nearly slamming into the house. Kyler shook his head, jogging behind.

"Calm down, ya brute. Inside. Go on." He reached over the massive animal and held the door open.

Murphy ran inside but abruptly stopped and sniffed the air.

"What'daya smell, boy? Go on. Kitchen."

Murphy was not allowed in the carpeted parts of the rental house, but the dog hunched down in refusal.

"Murphy, kitchen!"

Murphy snorted as he slowly padded to the kitchen, where Kyler filled a water dish and barred the doorway with chairs.

"Stay quiet, will ya? If you want to eat, I gotta keep my job, big guy."

Murphy cocked his head and gazed at him.

"You know how it is. G'night, Murph."

Kyler left Murphy in the kitchen and sauntered back upstairs. It had been a long day, but tomorrow would be much better. On his lunch break, he would take all that money to the bank and pay the stack of late bills on his table. He would pay off his debts, too, and start fresh. With his new job at the boatyard, life was finally going to get back to normal.

It was not just Kyler who was suffering, of course. The national economy had taken a turn for the worse. The beach seemed the most hard-pressed though. Local livelihoods depended on three things: the real estate market, the constant building, and the tourism. People were saving their money by not vacationing to the Outer Banks, and no one, not a soul, was building. Every other house on every street had a "For Sale" sign stuck in the sand in front of it. Builders were going bankrupt right and left. As a construction subcontractor, Kyler had gone weeks at a time without work.

There was work to do at Dartmouth's Yachts though. The folks who had the kind of money to buy one of those were not going to suffer with the tide of the economy. Besides, it took months to build just one yacht. Kyler was lucky enough to know a guy who knew a guy and ended up one of the last men hired this time around. The work was back breaking, but he didn't care.

He had also sold his pickup truck. He recalled his conversation with Old Man Southern that morning still somewhat in disbelief.

"I know ya work hard and ya work fair. I hate to see good folk strugglin' in these hard times," the old man had said to him at Peggy's breakfast joint. "How much ya owe on yer truck?"

Kyler watched the old man shake salt over his pile of grits until it seemed he'd emptied the shaker. He looked down at his own untouched breakfast. The familiar sounds of clanking dishes and chatter of Peggy's seemed deafening for some reason. He cleared his throat and tried to talk above the noise.

"Eight yet. I'm only asking the pay off. I wouldn't even ask that much if–"

"It's worth more than that. Tell ya what." The old man scooped a heaping bite into his mouth and talked through it. "I'll give ya ten."

Kyler shifted in his seat and felt his heart begin to race.

"I want ta help ya out, and this wud. Sides, I need me a truck that doesn't smell like crabbin' so the missus will ride round with me." He chuckled and slurped down some hot coffee.

"I-I don't know what..."

"Not a problem, son. It's the right thing to do. You a religious man?"

His cheeks felt hot. What had God ever done for him? The only good that ever came to him was what he earned himself through hard work, except this unexpected kindness. If there was a God, he had never seen any proof of it in this world, till now at least.

He shook his head, hoping it was not the wrong answer to give the old man. "Nothing in life is free, Jim. But luck? I believe in that. Sometimes I'm lucky. Sometimes I ain't. I just hope for the best."

"I never been much for superstition myself, but I think the good Lord watches out for us, I do."

"Well, thank *you* for watching out for me. You don't know how much this means to me. Really. I don't even know what to say."

An hour later, standing in the old man's driveway, Kyler had watched him count out the raggedy one hundred-dollar bills from the bottom of a fishing tackle box. The old fisherman must have money hidden away in more strange places than anyone would guess.

Jim eyed him. "You got a safe place to put this?"

"Yessir."

"Pleasure doing business with ya, son."

Afterward, as Kyler had walked south down the lone stretch of beach feeling warm and revived despite the wet chill outside, he had passed by a crew of young men in dirty jeans hauling boards of drywall up the stairs of a new beachfront house.

One man he recognized turned to notice him, but Kyler glanced away. He felt guilty. He could have smiled or waved or even stopped.

Before the economy dipped, Milo had been his only employee for months. He had to let him go when the opportunity came up at Dartmouth's. The boy was a good worker and quick to learn. They would have been successful in the business if times had stayed good. He hoped Milo would make it through the winter well enough.

At least Milo was on a job, Kyler thought. There was nothing he could do for the boy now. Everyone fended for themselves.

Kyler set his knife on the nightstand and gave his wallet one more satisfied glance. He eased onto the bed, falling back to sleep before he had time to kick off his boots.

Thump. Ruuf!

Murphy.

"Heeey!" Kyler slurred in anger, jostled from sleep. "You shut up!"

What time was it? Kyler rolled his sticky eyes toward the nightstand. His wallet blocked his view of the hour.

It wasn't important. His body relaxed back into the sheet.

Thump.

Wait a minute.

Thump.

That was coming from somewhere close.

Thump.

Not the kitchen. Was that…?

Thump.

It was footsteps coming up the stairs. Kyler's eyes shot open.

Thump.

Was that only half way up? How much time did he have? Murphy was barking and snarling downstairs, but Kyler knew the dog couldn't get out of the kitchen.

Thump.

He reached wildly for his knife and knocked it to the floor in the darkness.

Thump.

There was no time. Kyler sprang from the bed.

Thump.

The last step. He could sense the presence of another just around the corner in the stairwell. In a blind rush, he charged.

Wham.

Something hard smacked Kyler across his face. Staggering backward, he stumbled over a pile of clothes. Then the intruder was on him pinning him down. Kyler used all of his strength to try to free his arms from under the weight but he couldn't.

An iron fist smashed into his face. Again. And again.

His kicking feet felt the bed suddenly, and he pushed with all of his might. Enough of his body slid out from under his attacker to free his right arm, which he pummeled into a thick stomach. The impact jarred the intruder forward for another blow from Kyler. This time to his face.

Just as he thought he had gained the upper hand, Kyler heard the unmistakable snap of a knife opening. Searing pain shot into his shoulder.

"*Augh!*"

The knife ripped back out of his flesh. He felt the man raise an arm to pound it in again. To Kyler's shock, his own hand caught the attacker's arm in midair. The knife still came down with the tip puncturing his chest at the base of his neck. How far had it gone in? Sensing his attacker's surprise Kyler threw him off in a display of strength, but the attacker recovered in an instant and lunged.

Kyler managed to elude the grasp in time to dart into the adjacent bathroom. He slammed and locked the door. The attacker pounded into it from the other side attempting to bust through.

What was going on?! He needed a weapon.

Kyler opened the bathroom window and shimmied out onto the porch roof. He took cautious steps sideways across the steep boards toward the darker part of the yard and then jumped to the ground below with a jarring thud, and rolled.

"Yo!"

To his shock, a man's voice shouted from close by in the yard. Was there more than one of these guys? He desperately sucked air into his lungs and staggered to his feet.

"Yo! He's getting away!"

Kyler was up and running before the accomplice who had been waiting in the darkness gained on him. He had to be bleeding, but maybe he could hide once he got out of the new man's reach.

"Yo!"

He heard swift, heavy footsteps and huffing just behind him. Kyler ran around the house and plummeted himself out onto the street.

"You better get him!" The first attacker had now come out of the house. He shouted at his accomplice as he joined in the chase. Kyler ran until he saw a patch of thick, black trees to his right.

In a flash, he veered into their shadows. The man behind him darted in too, but Kyler jolted to a stop behind a thick trunk and stooped down.

The accomplice stopped and spun around in confusion gasping for breath.

The other attacker caught up. "Where'd he go?"

"I don't see him no more, man," said the breathless one.

An eruption of curse words.

Kyler slowly moved away, retreating deeper into the trees. He couldn't see the men, so he hoped they couldn't see him.

"What happened?"

"He was awake. I tried to knock him out."

"Did he see you?"

"I dunno."

More cursing.

"Yo, we have to find him. We get rid of him before he rats or–"

"Hold up. You want to *off* this guy?"

"I got him. He's hurt bad. If he saw me, we're goin' to prison."

More cursing.

"Man, let's just go get the money and get outta here."

"Are you a punk now? What's wrong with you? We get the money when we get *him*."

"You dun even know if he–"

"You're wasting my time. If you want paid then–"

"Naw. I'm out, man!"

The two men bickered darkly, shoving back and forth.

Kyler slowly inched away. When the voices were far enough behind him, he broke into a dash through the patch of woods. The next street couldn't be far.

One of the attacker's voices carried on the wind from the distance. "This way," he said.

Eventually, Kyler slowed to a trot. Was he safe? In a small clearing he dropped to the ground to catch his breath.

They knew about the money. He thought of his overflowing wallet on the nightstand, and anger flickered through him.

He could guess they were young. They were panicking. They were desperate. Nearly everyone on the beach was desperate. It could be anyone.

As he sat still and his nerves began to calm, a great heaviness came over him. He was painfully aware of the stab wound in his shoulder. Wet blood glued his t-shirt to the spot. He had no feeling in his arm and shoulder, but the gash throbbed with each heartbeat. The place on his neck felt just as hot and swollen, and he knew his eyes and lip were swelling.

He was dizzy. Very dizzy.

In the distance through the trees, he could make out four rectangular pillars of orange light standing side by side. It perplexed him for a moment until he realized. Those were the windows of a church building. Probably that old one at the deadend of Shell Street. Now he knew where he was. And church might actually come in handy for once.

You a religious man, son? Old Man Southern's voice slipped into his thoughts, just for a moment.

Crawling through brush, briers and small fallen timbers, Kyler pulled himself into what seemed to be a path in the trees. The church building came into view ahead.

He stood and crept forward, keeping the orange light in his now blurring vision. The ground was level so far. Finally coming to an opening, a large field dotted with dark tombstones was all that separated from him the building. It stood at the far end like a fortress rising to meet the black sky.

Above his head, clouds swirled rapidly without a star in sight. The light pouring from the church windows revealed an iron fence with a gate which the attackers would have to climb to get inside the churchyard. Surely, he would hear them if they did, and he would have time to hide.

Suddenly, Kyler felt his eyes roll back into his head. He swayed as he lost his balance and staggered forward. His foot caught in a dip of the earth, and he fell to the ground. If he stayed here, he could pass out. He had to get to the building.

Struggling to stand again, another wave of dizziness washed through him. This time, he fell onto his wounded shoulder and uttered a small cry with clenched teeth. The pain was worse. Throbbing.

Just then, a bolt of lightning streaked across the sky. It illuminated the yard to reveal that both the church building and the old, unkempt cemetery where Kyler lay were surrounded by beds of long, green leaves and topped with yellow flower balls. The flower petals shone, reflecting traces of moonlight that had escaped the dark clouds. Their thick stems rose nearly two feet into the air. They looked familiar. Had he been here before?

Yes. His dream. The field. The storm. And even these flowers. What did it mean?

There was no time to contemplate. To his dismay, Kyler heard a clanking sound. He could just make out the form of a man scampering over the gate. The attackers must have known he would run toward the lit building.

He considered making a run for it, but he couldn't risk the men getting to him first. He would have to hide. He heaved himself into a mass of the bushy flower leaves hoping their fullness might conceal him. All he could do was … was…

No. He couldn't pray. Where had God been when the economy was sucking him dry? Where had God been for anything else in his life, in fact?

Are you a religious man?

Luck did not seem to be on his side tonight. For the first time since he was a boy, he decided he would try.

"God?" He whispered, wincing at his awkwardness. "Jesus? I could use some help. I know I ain't been… living like I should. I'm sorry about that. But if you're really there, I need you to save my life. It's gonna have to be you… Please."

Another streak of lightning raced across the sky. He saw for a moment a hollow-eyed, stone angel staring down at him from a nearby tombstone.

Kyler held his breath and listened. It was not long before he heard them approach.

"Man, he ain't here. He's at the police station by now."

"Yo, shut up! We ain't givin' up like that."

"It's going to start rainin', man."

"Gimmie your phone."

"What for?"

"I need a light."

Their footsteps crunched through the tall, dry grass nearby.

"You dun understand man," the more confidant man was saying. "This guy told me work would pick up. He just screwed me one day, man. He left me with nothin'. Then I come to find out from my boy that Old Man Southern gave him ten G's. He ain't called me to offer me any help or nothin'. He knows I'm hurting bad. I can't believe he would do me like this."

Milo. It was Milo, but it didn't sound like him. He sounded sinister.

"I see something."

Kyler knew the beam of a light was on his face before he opened his eyes.

Hoots of cursing filled the air as the two young men yanked Kyler's aching body out of the flowers. He heard Milo snap open his knife again.

"Wait," his accomplice objected. Milo ignored him.

"Sup Ky! You thought you could hide. You hurt bad, punk, but you gonna be worse off than that."

"I heard somethin'," said the other.

They stopped.

"You better not be messin' wit me," Milo barked.

"Listen."

At once, Kyler heard it, too.

Voices.

"Go check it out," Milo said to the other in a low voice. "He's not getting away again." Milo picked Kyler's head up by his hair and shoved it into the ground. "*You* don't make a sound."

Kyler lay still. Milo towered above him rigidly. Both strained their ears.

Just then, a gust of wind surged through the trees behind them and filled the grassy cemetery. There was a rise of murmuring voices from all around. It had to be a swarm of people. All whispering. All talking at once. They must have come from the church building. With another burst of wind, they grew louder, closer. They were right there.

Milo released him in an instant. Kyler's heart swelled with relief.

"Yo! Let's go!"

Kyler heard the sound of their footsteps racing away in panic. He lifted his head expecting to see dozens of people standing around him. As he peered around the churchyard, another bolt of lightning flashed in the sky.

There was no one.

All he saw before consciousness faded away were the bright yellow petals of the tall flowers bobbing in the wind above his head.

When the first hot drops of rain began to fall through the sultry air soon after, Sheriff Conoway nudged Kyler's good shoulder.

"Are you alright, son?"

Kyler opened his eyes to slits.

"The ambulance is on the way."

The sheriff helped him sit up. He hurt all over.

"Yep. Somebody is looking out for you," the sheriff said. He glanced at the church building. Kyler vaguely noticed that the lights were off. "My officer said he was coming by here to check things out since there was a light inside. He suspected maybe some kids were foolin' round. This church has been empty for years. I was already up and about, so I met him."

Kyler tried to form words in spite of his dry mouth. "That's why I tried to come here. The light."

"That so?" The sheriff looked thoughtful. "By the time we arrived, the church was dark, but two roughians were tearing up over the fence quick as lightnin'. They were so spooked, they told us everything."

"Milo."

"Yessir. Milo Chesney and Brian O'Donnell. Officer Turner took them in. Are you a superstitious man, son?"

"What do you mean?"

"Beings that you're holding onto that flower for dear life, I thought maybe you was."

Kyler looked down to see his own hands clutching one of the big balls of petals. He tossed it away.

"You'll see betony growing in all old churchyards. They say it keeps evil spirits out."

The image of Milo and Brian climbing the gate to come after him flashed into Kyler's mind.

"No, sheriff, not me," he said.

"Well, perhaps it wasn't a flower that helped you, but somethin' did."

"How do you figure?"

"Oh, this old church building has never had power running to it. If it weren't for the light, you would not have come here, you say. The same way, we never would have come. And what do you suppose spooked those boys? They thought they was surrounded by folks, but there's nobody here. I reckon if it weren't ghosts, it sure musta been something supernatural. They do say God works in mysterious ways."

Kyler blinked and looked over at the old church building.

"I reckon," he said.

A Letter for Moonbeam

*A German knight was once gathering a bouquet of blue wildflowers
near a waterside for his beloved. Suddenly, a flash flood came and
pulled him into the river. Before vanishing under the water, he
tossed the flowers to the bank crying, "Forget me not!"
Thus, the Forget Me Nots received their name.*

IT WAS THE biggest decision of my life, and I was running out of time.

Moonlight poured through the window. Everyone in the manor slept except for me and my mother's portrait that smiled from above the mantel. I wished more than ever that I could talk to her.

I couldn't talk to the rest of my family, either. Aunt Sarah was not the kind of woman for heart-to-hearts. When Mother had died, Aunt Sarah provided me with tutors and textbooks like a proper Burton. For all she knew, Jake Pearson was an acceptable match, and I should marry him tomorrow. For once, I wondered if she was right.

Jill had only made things worse. My cousin was usually the

only reasonable person in my life, yet she thought it was a good idea to tell me Michael Kennedy was back town, *looking for me*. She had bumped into him at a fueling station. Her words burned in my mind. His words.

She's the one that got away.

"Maybe you should talk to him, Theo," she had said. "It might help you."

I kicked off the bedcovers in frustration. This was not my bed. I couldn't sleep suctioned-cupped by a cloud of down feathers. It was making me claustrophobic.

Everything in the Burton manor was grand and luxurious, but I was more familiar with the chic version of the Burton lifestyle. Aunt Sarah lived in a posh, white-walled apartment in the city. We did not have overstuffed pillows and lacy sheets. There was no decorative woodwork or strange, cloth wallpaper. Aunt Sarah liked angles and art. She had cactus plants, a white cat, and canvas paintings of what appeared to be splattered cocktail sauce. I never understood painting.

Although I was a Burton, too, I never had the impression any of the others wanted me to be. I was just a long-term guest in their lives, one that was an inconvenience ever since Mother died. I remembered little about my mother, but I knew she could not have been like them.

My wedding gown hung on the oval mirror next to the dressing table. It looked different in the night, like a floating, white ghost. I shuddered.

Well, since I didn't have a mother tonight, or anything close to it, I would have to settle for visiting the places where I remembered her best.

I rolled twice to reach the end of the bed and slid my legs over the edge. My toes grazed the cold, hardwood floor. Then the rest of me plopped out with a graceless thud.

This room had been Mother's. Grandmother transformed it into a guest room many years ago, as if she didn't have enough of those already. All that remained of my mother in here was her portrait. The artist had given her the wrong mouth but had captured her eyes just the way I remembered them. Kind and sparkling like blue stars.

Another room in the manor reminded me of Mother much better.

I tiptoed to the door and slowly opened it. It let out a soft creak. In the hall, other portraits lined the walls and sheer drapes moved in the summer breeze from cracked windows.

Jill was in the room next to mine. Grandmother and Aunt Sarah stayed in rooms down the hall in the front of the manor. Jake and his Best Man were in another building on the property. I ambled toward the old servant's quarters in the back. Toward the nursery.

When I slipped into the room, my feet sunk in the plush carpet. The place was illuminated in blue-gray moonlight. My eyes drifted over the ornate fireplace, the shelves of unblinking dolls and wooden toys, and the tiny table ever set for tea. I looked up at the mobile hanging low from the center of the ceiling. Smiling stars and clouds cascaded down from a large, equally happy moon.

"Moonbeam," I whispered.

When I was a child, my favorite nursery rhyme was The Man in The Moon. Mother recited it with me every night before bed. My chest pinched at the memory.

At least the nursery had never been remodeled. All plantation manors retained one. As a result, all the old books had survived. They were all that remained now of my earliest childhood.

I went to the bookshelf and reached for the thickest volume. It was the old, worn book of nursery rhymes that Mother read to me. The cover had once been white; at least that's what I thought. It was beige now, and the pages, though still bound together, were coming detached from the spine in one heap. It had been that way from the time I could remember.

The smell of the book reminded me of her. I breathed it in, letting the pain resurface.

Mother had only been sick for a few months before she went to sleep for good. We lived with Grandmother during that time. Afterward, Aunt Sarah had whisked me away to her place in Richmond. Most of my things disappeared in the transition. Mother had already added our books to the nursery at Trinity Hall. She must have known they would be preserved that way.

I sat down in the rocking chair. Tiny pieces of the book cover flaked into my lap as the pages fell open easily to where flowers, now squished and dried and forgotten, had been placed in the crease. I smiled, touching the small, dark petals. I wondered if I had put them there, or Mother.

I bit my lip as my eyes scanned the words on the page.

The man in the moon, looked out of the moon...

The light in the room became brighter as though a cloud had moved away.

"Is that you, Man in the Moon?" I asked.

Suddenly, the book pages came loose and slid deeper into my lap while the cover remained in my hands. My breath caught, but the dried flowers had stayed intact. As I tried to fix the book, I caught a glimpse of handwriting on the inside of the cover.

Moonbeam.

I quickly flipped it open.

This book is for you. Always be true to yourself and never stop believing. Love, Mom

I touched the handwriting. My mother's nickname for me.

I wanted to make her little piece of advice work for my current situation, but the longer I thought about it, the worse I felt. How could I be true to myself if I didn't know who I was? I had never been Theodora the Burton heiress in the way my aunt and grandmother thought I should be, no matter how much I had tried. I didn't want to be a debutante, to host dinner parties or pretend I was something I was not.

I wanted out. That's where Jake came in.

I would not marry someone I did not love, but marriage also meant getting out. It meant identifying myself with a new family name, one with fewer expectations and a less painful past. And someone to love me back. Marrying Jake not be the same as marrying Michael would have been. Jake would not take me away from the limelight. It would just be dimmer.

A tear slid down my cheek. The wedding would be the last big social event of my life. Aunt Sarah had seen to it that I hit every milestone with a celebration at the manor. When I refused a big wedding, they accepted no less than a ceremony and reception at the house rather than a quick to-do at a small church. I did not want the attention. I did not want my name in the news. I agreed only because it was the last time.

Then it would all be over.

How had my mother lived this life with such grace? Maybe that was just the way I remembered it. For the first time, I wondered how the rest of the family had reacted to my father leaving us. Had Mother been ashamed? Is that why we had lived in a small house on the beach until she got sick? This had never occurred to me before.

I shook my head.

"The man in the moon looked out of the moon..."

A breeze grazed my legs. I glanced up at the window in time to see the drapes settle back into place.

"Do you want to tell me something, man in the moon?"

I went to the window, book in hand. The courtyard below was surrounded by sculpted bushes that reminded me of creatures. Water trickled in the white marble fountain. These days, the poor naked woman posted atop it was missing pieces of her fingers, and she had a crack in her torso. Grandmother probably would have had her repaired or even replaced. Aunt Sarah was concerned with even more trivial details than that. White folding chairs were lined up exactly two inches apart from one another on either side of the walk, leaving an aisle exactly five feet across.

It wasn't marriage that frightened me. I just didn't want to walk down that aisle to the wrong groom.

Jake fit the bill for the Burton family. He was not wealthy like them, but he was known among them for his culinary accomplishments. I had met him at a dinner party that I wanted to escape. He let me take cover in the kitchen. We spent the evening sneaking peeks at the guests and making up hilarious scenarios about their lives. Jake made me laugh. He made me forget Michael. For a while.

Neither of us knew I still had feelings for Michael Kennedy, my previous boyfriend of two years who had vanished without an explanation. Not until Jake and I were engaged. Then I began to remember him.

I never knew why Michael had left me. One day, he had just packed up his things and told me he had to go back to his hometown. I couldn't go with him, but we were not breaking up, he had said. He just had some things he needed to take care of for a while. He had been communicating with me less and less. Once he was gone, he never called or answered his phone. He just vanished. Friends of friends eventually told me he was fine and still writing music. I was devastated.

I had thought I would marry Michael. He had a motorcycle, long hair and tattoos. Nothing like clean-cut Jake. Or anyone else in the Burton circles. He played the guitar and wrote his own songs. Aunt Sarah had been horrified. The more horrified she was, the more I had liked him. He had lost his mother, too. And he was free. He dared me to live just as free. We spent days and nights sprawled on the beach under the stars. When I was with him, I forgot all about the Burton family paradigm.

I waited for Michael to come back for a long time, but he never did. When I met Jake, I finally decided to let go. Jake made it easy enough. But Jill's news had stunned me. Of all times for Michael to come back and want to talk, why did he have to pick the day before my wedding? As if I didn't have enough to think about, all of the memories of my time with him came surging back.

If I did talk to Michael, and he had a good reason for leaving, and he still loved me, what would I do?

I closed my eyes. "The man in the moon looked out of the moon, looked out of the moon and said…"

Another slight gust of wind fluttered the drapes at my ankles. Beyond the courtyard, the moon cast an even brighter light. I could see the path that curled around the pond. Mother and I had our picnics there. A weeping willow tree mounted up from the ground and reached over the water with its umbrella. I could even make out speckles of tiny wildflowers along the bank. Were they the same kind as the pressed flowers in the book?

I suddenly wanted to know. No. I *had* to know. I imagined my mother standing in the grass picking the flowers so many years ago. For Moonbeam.

I took the book with me. Tiptoeing through the manor and out the front door, I slid into the moonlit evening that was far brighter out of doors. The manor was asleep, but outside, the night had bloomed to life. My silk nightgown skimmed across my skin in the breeze. The cool grass hugged my bare feet.

I followed the cobblestone path to the pond. On the bank, I opened the book again. Whatever these wildflowers were, they were the same as the pressed ones. They were coin-sized, blue blossoms with yellow centers and entwined together with vein-like stems.

My mother had perhaps stood in this very spot either with or thinking of me. She had probably done it hundreds of times, but just knowing she did sent warmth through me like a hug. What had she seen in these plain, tiny flowers? Did she know I would find them again one day?

I looked up at the moon. The nearby trees almost pierced his belly. He stared down at me stone-faced, a perfect sphere. A dull blue emitted from him.

"The man in the moon looked out of the moon, looked out of the moon and said…" I imagined his oblong mouth opening. "It's time for all children on the Earth to think about getting to bed."

I put a hand on my hip. "Well," I said, "I'm not a child, and I can't sleep." But he just smiled. "You're not any help, are you?"

The blue haze enveloped him, and he cast the place in a sapphire hue as though I was looking through a lens.

Suddenly, the book pages slipped out of the cover again. I tightened my grip before they fell. The dried flowers didn't come loose, but the pointy edge of a piece of folded notebook paper protruded from the middle of the book. What was this?

I quickly unfolded the paper. Right away, I saw it contained more of my mother's handwriting. A letter! My heart raced. Just as I spotted the name, I caught a glimpse of a shadow. Someone stood behind me.

I gasped, spinning around.

"Moonbeam," said a woman.

She wore a long white dress with her bare feet poking out from under the hem. She had dark hair that cascaded down in waves around her face and curves. Her eyes were as I remembered, and so was her full-lipped, smiling mouth.

I seemed to be held up by invisible hands. My body felt loose and wobbly like I should be crumpled on the ground. I must have dropped the book and letter because later, I did not remember holding them anymore.

Mother held out her arms to me, but I couldn't move.

"I…I don't understand," I managed to say.

Her skin had an ethereal bluish light to it, even more than anything else draped in the moon's hue. She stepped forward. She touched my shoulder with one hand and cupped my chin in her other. I winced, thinking her touch would be icy or non-existent, like a ghost. It was warm and real.

"I may be gone now," she said in her voice. My mother's voice. "But I hope the memory of me has stayed with you." She never stopped smiling.

I wanted to tell her I did remember her, but I knew I didn't remember all the way. I had only been four years old. Guilt clenched my heart. My silence began to draw out. She didn't seem to notice. If I spoke, would she vanish? What would happen if I *didn't*?

At some point, I noticed a tingling sensation moving through me, and I thought I might be floating. Then all at once, it all felt as natural as life. My dead mother stood right there, and it was as normal as if I had spoken to her like this thousands of times. What was happening? It didn't matter.

"Mother, I miss you," I blurted. My voice sounded loud and harsh as it pricked the stillness. Maybe I shouldn't talk after all. I should just listen to her and look at her and feel her. Why was she was so small? It was strange to be her height now and able to stare into her eyes. I finally remembered my limp arms and tentatively reached out to touch her waist, inches from mine. Her form felt soft and alive beneath my trembling fingers. She took another step forward and encircled me in her arms. Her cheek brushed mine. My head reeled. I closed my eyes. She smelled like memories.

"I hope you know how much I love you," she said in my ear. Her embrace tightened. "I hope you remember all the things we did together. We were inseparable. The best of friends." She laughed. It was her laugh, just the way I remembered.

She pulled back slightly still in my arms, smiled at me again, and touched my face again. I couldn't remember anyone ever looking at me with that much love. She motioned to the grass and pulled me down to sit with her. We sat with our legs crossed and our knees touching. A frog hopped into the water somewhere, making a tiny, distant splash.

"I'm sorry I wasn't around to see you grow up," she said, "but I know you have become a remarkable young woman. I'm so very proud of you. After all, you are a Burton."

I didn't want to look away, but it was a habit. I had never done anything like a real Burton. I just didn't fit the mold. It was like being stuck in a boat without paddles and expected to travel upstream. I just wasn't made with what I needed. My picture could be in the dictionary next to the word *ordinary*.

She reached out and gently pulled my face back. "Don't worry," she said, very serious. "It's not the name that makes you a Burton. You belong in this family because that is where God put you. He made you exactly as you are for a reason."

A lump formed in my chest. It rose up my throat faster than I could stop it, and at once, the tears filled my eyes. I wanted to tell her the truth even if she was disappointed. I wanted to talk to my mother.

"I think there's something wrong with me," I whimpered, admitting it out loud for the first time. "I never do anything right. It doesn't feel like I belong. I don't know what to do. If I marry Jake, I may have to go on being an embarrassment to everybody around me for the rest of my life." Heat rose into my cheeks. Even if the moon did not shield the blush, I didn't care. The shame was not nearly so bad in that moment.

My mother just smiled and nodded as though there was a solution for my pain.

"Your family and everyone around you needs you to be who God created you to be," she said. "So don't let anyone tell you who you are *supposed* to be."

Who had God created me to be? That was the million dollar question.

"Whatever your interests are, fly with them," she continued. "Dream big and have faith. Most of all, it's important that you always stay true to yourself."

There it was again.

"Stay true to what?" I heard myself say. "If you mean staying true to my failures, I'm good at that." It sounded dumb out loud.

She gazed at me, eyes shining. "You are beautiful, strong and good enough because God says you are. *He* has the final say on you."

Could that be true beyond the God-talk that people wrote in cards to say something special? I felt a new kind of lump swell inside me. I *wanted* to believe her. Beautiful, she had said. Strong. Good Enough. How wonderful that all sounded. But if this was a dream, could I ever let myself believe her?

Maybe for a just a little while.

"And it's okay to make mistakes," she went on. "Just dust yourself off and get back up again. God will uphold you, if you let Him."

Mistakes.

"Mother," I said quickly. I couldn't believe I was going to get to ask her what to do. "I don't want to make any more mistakes. At least not big, important ones. I'm getting married tomorrow." She nodded as though she knew. "I love Jake. So much. But there's another man, maybe. At least, there used to be. I don't know what happened, but I've always wanted to understand. He wants to talk to me now, but what kind of person would I be if I talk to him *now*? I mean, what would Jake think? I feel so confused. What if this is all happening because Michael was the one after all? Mother, when a man is the one I'm supposed to marry, how do I know?"

Her forehead creased. She took one of my hands in both of hers. My other hand made a fist around a clump of grass blades anxious for her words of wisdom. If anyone could tell me what to do, I knew my mother could. I just knew it. That's what mothers do.

"I'm sure you've wondered about your father," she began. My breath caught. I hadn't expected that, but of course it made sense. Was I finally going to get to know what happened? No one had ever talked about it. They always changed the subject when I asked.

"I think it would be easiest if I tell you a story." She turned her head and gave the moon a faraway look. "Once upon a time, there lived a young girl whose parents kept her so busy that she hardly had time to play. She had many responsibilities, and if she wanted to get into the very best schools, she had to study all day, every day." The Burton way. She looked back at me. "One day, the girl met a young man who was very handsome, and he wanted to spend time with her. He did not like her strict schedule any more than she did. He prodded her until she finally consented to start sneaking out at night, skipping lessons and lying to her family just to see him."

My mouth hung open. I couldn't imagine my mother being anything but an obedient daughter. She smiled.

"The boy told her that he loved her, but he didn't like her family. He asked her to run away from them. To be with him. The things that he told her about her family made sense to her. Something inside of her made her feel uneasy, but she ignored it and did what he asked. After she ran away, the boy was not the same. He hardly ever came home and was not very nice to her anymore. It turned out that he didn't truly love her after all. He was more interested in himself. She would have known that by the way he treated her family, but she was so eager for a different life that she had not noticed. Where she belonged was where God had put her, with the ones who loved her."

My heart raced. It was like she was telling my own story.

"One day, the young girl found out she was expecting a baby. You can guess what happened. The boy left her, of course. But it was a good thing because he would not have been a loving father. The young girl and her daughter were much happier without him." She stopped, smiled and patted my hand. "But she hoped one day her own little girl would listen to that voice inside of her and *stay true to herself.* Whether or not you always like being a Burton, that is who you were made to be. And the man you fall in love with is only worthy of you if he loves God and loves you for who you are, and if he is honest and works hard to take care of you. If he's not those things, you will know it deep down inside. You will also know deep inside if he *is.*"

I shook my head. Mother deserved so much better than what my father had done to her. At least she knew it. Thank God she knew it.

"I'm so sorry, Mother. I'm so sorry you went through that."

She leaned in to hug me, and I met her in the middle. "God has an amazing story written for you," she murmured. "You will find heartbreak at times and face big challenges. Sometimes you will feel confused and let down. But God, who is your real Father, and a perfect and loving one, will always be there for you."

God being my Father was not a foreign idea to me, but I had never really thought about it before. I liked it. I mulled over the concept in my mind.

"But I don't feel close to him," I said, pulling back.

She nodded. "It's important that you let Him into your heart so He *can* be your Father. That way, you will always know who you are, and it will be easy to stay true to yourself. You will know where you belong."

To belong somewhere had always eluded me. I couldn't change my roots, and I certainly didn't fit into Aunt Sarah's vision for me. But I wanted to belong. I did.

As though reading my thoughts, she said, "It will be hard growing up a Burton, but have patience with your aunt. She only wants what's best for you, and she has her own way of showing it. Remember, your choices are your own. They are not so difficult as they seem."

I opened my mouth to object, but she said, "I know you will always do the right thing. I have faith in you."

Her skin seemed to glow an even deeper shade of blue. She grasped my hands and stood up, pulling me up with her. Was she leaving? I clung to her waist. She ran her fingers through my hair.

"I wish I could be there for your wedding," she whispered. "And to see your own little ones. But I believe we will be together again one day. If you let God be your Father, He will give you that peace, too."

"Mother, please don't leave," I said. I realized I was crying again. After a long moment, I saw that she had left my embrace. I didn't remember letting go.

"I'll be waiting for you, Moonbeam," she said, smiling very big, her eyes crinkling at the corners.

"No, wait," I reached for her, but I couldn't move. My body felt heavy again and supported only by the invisible hands.

"Always remember me and how much I love you," she said.

The blue enfolded her. For an odd moment, I thought to myself that it was the same shade as Jake's eyes.

I don't know what happened next.

I awoke in the morning. The sun poured into my mother's room and reflected off my gown. I sat up in the bed shielding my eyes.

No moon. No mother. Her portrait smiled at me with the wrong mouth.

I looked down and saw the book of nursery rhymes and Mother's letter lying in the fluffy sheets next to me. The letter was for me, I remembered. "Moonbeam," it had started. My eyes scanned the pages and then drifted over the last lines.

Always remember me and how much I love you. Love, Mom

A sharp rapping on the door jarred me from my thoughts.

"Rise and shine," sang Jill as she burst into the room. "Are you ready?"

You will know deep inside…Your choices are you own. And they are not so difficult as they seem.

A few hours later, I waited on the porch with Jill. My gown swished on the flagstone as I paced back and forth. The rose-colored dress we had chosen for Jill hugged her just right, too. I felt so much better now that I had prayed to God that morning asking Him to be my Father, just like I know my mother had done. And just like she said that He would, He had given me peace.

Any minute now, the wedding coordinator would come to get us. The guests were likely all seated, and the final song of the prelude from the string ensemble drifted through the air.

I never heard him approach.

"Hey, Theo," said a deep voice behind me.

I saw Jill's eyes bulge before I turned. I already knew who it was.

His hair hung to his shoulders, and his T-shirt flapped against his lean body. He looked like a sheet of paper compared to muscular Jake. It took me off guard. He wore his old smug smile as he bounced up the stone stairs, his flip flops smacking the slabs. He propped an arm on a column like he belonged there and could do what he wanted.

"Michael," I said.

"How are you doing, sweet girl?"

"I'm getting married, Michael. In a few minutes."

He stretched out his arms toward me, palms up. "And look how beautiful you are."

"Thanks…"

His grin faded a little. "You do. You're gorgeous." He said it as though it was a realization he unexpectedly stumbled upon. He might as well have added, "Huh. Isn't that something? I never would have thought."

The music in the courtyard ended. The song for my aunt and Jake's mother to walk down the aisle began to play.

"Why are you here?" I asked.

He lowered his eyes. The moment I had wanted for years was here, but now it didn't even matter.

"Michael, if there's something you want to say, say it."

He nodded. "I know I shouldn't have come," he said, wringing his hands. "But I couldn't help it. I regret losing you, Theo. I think about it every day. You're the girl I was supposed to be with. You were my once in a lifetime shot." He raised his head. His eyes found mine, and he took a tremendous breath. "I love you, Theo."

Before the previous night, I might not have known what to do.

"Where were you?" I asked.

His eyes darted away. I knew they would. "I don't know. What do you want to hear? I made a lot of mistakes. I'm sorry."

"But what were you doing?"

He shoved his hands into his pockets. "Apparently all the wrong stuff, okay? I never should have left. I thought I had a shot at a record deal. I wasn't ready to settle down. I was young and stupid. I know better now. I would never leave you if I could do it again. I really do love you."

"Okay, ladies!"

Sandy, my sister's most trusted event planner, appeared from around the corner. She clapped her chubby, manicured hands. "Let's go, it's time!"

Jill looked from her to me with her eyebrows raised.

"I have to go, Michael. I'm sorry," I said, sweeping past him. "Oh, but Michael?" I turned back. His grin had reemerged. "I believe everything happens for a reason. Don't worry. This is the way it's supposed to be, for both of us."

As Jill and I followed Sandy, disappearing from Michael's view around the corner of the house, Jill slung an arm around my shoulders and kissed my cheek. "I'm so proud of you," she said. And then a second later, "Ohh, lookie there." She pointed to a patch of the small blue wildflowers hiding in the grass at the base of a bush. "These are called Forget Me Nots," she said, scampering over to pluck a few. She tucked one deep into my bouquet. "Something *blue*!"

When I stepped into the entrance of the courtyard, I looked straight ahead. A pair of soft, blue eyes met mine. Jake smiled. All was as it should be.

THE STORY

EVELYN NEWBELL

TOLD

Of all wildflowers, St. John's Wort has an especially long lore attached to it. In the first century, legend tells us that Christians named it for John the Baptist. The yellow blossoms usually appear on or before June 24th, which the Church celebrates as his birthday. The plant also exudes a crimson red liquid, symbolizing John's spilled blood, or Christ's. St. John's Wort was sometimes woven into wreaths to keep the devil at bay. Many cultures use it to this day as an exorcist for demons. The flower has long been used to treat illnesses of the mind, such as anxiety, depression and memory loss. It has also been said to be able to foretell the time of a young woman's marriage and to predict the lucky groom.

EVELYN NEWBELL, called Evie, first told this story when she was five years old. Not many believed her then, or the many times afterward that she repeated it, until Hugh Thomas, called Hughey by her, asked her to accompany him to their tenth-grade school dance. Then people started to pay attention. When Evie later married *Hughey* and became Evelyn Thomas, hardly anyone doubted her anymore.

Evie's story happened in the summer of year of the world-wide solar flare in a quiet mountain community of rural Pennsylvania. There, backyards melted into the forest, and simple grocery shopping for residents required a daytrip to town. Evie lived in town, but her *Grammie* lived in the mountains.

It was Independence Day weekend. Evie's family would be attending a picnic at Aunt Lois' house. Aunt Lois lived down the lane from Grammie. Everyone called Aunt Lois *Aunt Lois*, including Evie, even though Aunt Lois was not everyone's aunt. Some of them never knew it. She was, however, Daddy and Aunt Jen's aunt.

Aunt Lois was different from Grammie. She always spoke her mind, played her music too loud and told the younger family members all the worst stories about the older ones. She was a walking bible of old wive's tales and knew all the local secrets. If you had a question and you didn't mind a peculiar answer as long as it was true, you asked Aunt Lois.

That afternoon, Daddy and Aunt Jen were sitting at Grammie's kitchen table with *the paperwork*. Evie's Pappy had passed away before Grammie's dementia diagnosis. Shriver Newbell, called *Baldy* by everyone else, had owned a trash disposal company that he had started up after retiring from the steel mill. According to him, selling the company, or selling assets truck by truck, would provide for Grammie once he was gone. Pappy had never dealt with the company ledger books himself. That had always been Grammie's job.

Evie's Daddy, whose name was Lawrence, and his sister, Evie's

Aunt Jen, were the first to realize Pappy must have known about Grammie's illness long before they did. The ledgers were in complete disarray. For them, figuring out the company's true worth and preparing to sell it was a debacle. Stacks of paper, ledger books, receipts and bills were sprawled endlessly before the brother and sister on Grammie's kitchen table every weekend.

Back in Grammie's bedroom, Evie sat next to Grammie on a cushioned stool facing an old dressing table mirror. Pappy had found the dressing table with the long mirror speckled with remnants of old stickers on the garbage run, the same with most of Grammie's trinkets.

Evie's reflection in the mirror looked just as you would expect. She had straight, golden hair and plump cheeks. But not Grammie's.

Instead of old Grammie, staring back at them from the mirror was a young beauty with bright blue eyes and auburn hair caught neatly back with pins. A single candle's flame flickered on the young woman's dressing table, and a lovely stem of wildflower blossoms drank clear water from a glass vase. On this side of the mirror, a melted down, unlit candle sat in a pool of hard wax, and a brown, dry stem sagged in a yellowed vase.

It is said that young children have the ability to see the world through another's eyes. If you have ever wondered at a young child's empathy, this is the reason. It was not strange to Evie to see what her grandmother saw in the mirror. Not like it would be for grownups. For as long as Evie could remember, she had always seen the young woman in the mirror at Grammie's house.

The woman in the mirror smiled at Evie. The little girl absently plugged her thumb into her mouth. Now the mirror maiden's brow furrowed, and so did Grammie's.

"You know you're not supposed to do that anymore," Grammie said in her sweet voice, not really scolding, as she pulled out the thumb.

"Grammie," said Evie, feeling bored and noticing the sun shining in the window. "Can we go for a walk?"

Evie knew Grammie moved much slower now than before on account of her knees, but it never occurred to her that walking might be painful. It never occurred to Grammie to say so.

"A walk? Oh, sure. We can do that." Grammie began the difficult maneuvering to stand. The young woman in the mirror mimicked her every move.

Grammie's yard would one day become regular, and the forest would creep forward and begin to eat up the special spots that Evie knew so well. But today, it was timeless, and every walk at Grammie's was a wonderful adventure.

Evie tugged Grammie down the hall. They passed Daddy and Aunt Jen in the kitchen.

"We're going for a walk, Daddy," Evie called.

Daddy opened his mouth to object but decided fresh air for Grammie might be good. "Be careful and walk *slow*," he said.

When they went outside, Grammie asked, "Where to first?"

Evie tapped her chin with her finger. "Let's go to the fish pond."

Before Pappy's illness, catfish lips had bubbled to the surface of the pond water in search of the breadcrumbs that Evie would throw in for them. There were no fish now. Pappy had dug the pond out long ago, and now it didn't retain water like before. Daddy hadn't been able to figure out why. Now it just looked like a swamp choking on grass.

As they came upon the bank, Grammie said, "This pond has been here a long time, Evie. Your daddy and your aunt and so many other kids played here when they were your age." She looked across what was left of the water.

Evie later said that Grammie's eyes took on a misty look that day when she recalled her long ago memories. Although Evie had always seen the young woman in the mirror, she had never seen any of Grammie's other memories before.

All of a sudden, Evie heard children's laughter. The sound seemed to come from one direction at first and then from another. All at once, it burst from behind. She whirled around to see a boy no taller than herself charge passed them and splash into the water. It was suddenly quite deep. The grasses were gone, too.

"Libby," the boy said with a grin absent of his two front teeth. "Look at me!"

He crouched down in the pond and stuck out his tongue in concentration. In a moment, he sprang back up holding a wiggling catfish in both hands. The fish writhed and fought his captor, who squealed with laughter.

Probably more amazing to Evie than the appearance of the boy, and the water, and even the fish, was that for the first time in her life, Evie heard Grammie scold.

"Albert," said Grammie, putting her hands on her hips and sounding truly stern. "Albert, you put that down and get out of there now. You mother will have our hides!"

Like most little boys who add a twist to their obedience, before leaving the pond, this one threw the squirming fish high into the air. He howled with laughter as it entered the water again with a loud splat.

"Libby!"

Another voice came from nearby. This one belonged to a girl slightly taller than Evie. She had two waist-length, black braids. The girl suddenly stood just on the other side of Grammie.

"Do we have to let him change clothes? He should stay wet. Serves him right," the girl said.

Grammie shook her head. "Oh, come on, you two."

Evie heard the boy splashing toward them, but when she

turned back, he was gone. The girl had vanished, too, and the pond returned to its shabby state.

"Alice, hold your brother's hand," Grammie was saying. "Oh, what am I going to tell your moth-" Grammie's eyes met Evie's, and the mist disappeared. "Evie?...Oh, Evie... I was just thinking about my niece and nephew..."

Having heard many of Aunt Lois' stories, Evie wondered if she had just seen ghosts, but she was only curious and not frightened. Young children are rarely afraid of such things. But seeing how Grammie was so confused, Evie gently took her hand and began to lead her away. She was well-seasoned in caring for her often-confused grandmother. It was always best to move on to something else.

"Let's go this way, Grammie," Evie said.

The strawberry patch was not far from the pond. There had been strawberries last weekend, and Evie knew there would be more now. It was on the way to *the path between the wood*, as it was called by Daddy. The path between the wood bypassed the chicken coop and some untamed grasses on the way to the garden. Evie pulled Grammie along, looking back sometimes to see if the ghost children were following them.

As they approached the little strawberry patch, Evie let go of Grammie's hand. She ran ahead and plopped down amongst the plants. She was just reaching out to pluck a nice, juicy berry when a man's voice boomed.

"Rotten girls!"

Giggling erupted right in front of Evie. Two young women materialized, sitting in the center of the patch only a few feet away. They both wore floral dresses. Their lips were painted with bright red lipstick, and their dark hair was tightly curled against their heads. One whispered, "Look, there he is." They giggled again.

A lean, young man wearing a white, cotton shirt and brown pants with suspenders appeared in the distance stomping toward them, his arms swinging wildly.

"You girls quit lollygagging and do something useful around here!" he said. "Get up to the house and can those peaches!"

This sent the two women into another fit of laughter. They nudged one another and began to pick strawberries by the fistfuls and dump them into their basket. The man fumed but finally turned and stalked away, muttering under his breath.

"Shriver," one of the women called after him. "Your peaches are going to rot! You should can them yourself!" She hooted with laughter, delighted with herself. Then she glanced up and noticed Grammie, who was slowly making her way to the patch. Grammie looked strangely shy.

"Oh! Why, hello, Libby dear," the woman said.

"Hello," Grammie said, smiling a tiny, uncertain smile.

"Birdie, this is Libby from up the lane. She just moved here from West Virginia."

"That far?" Birdie said.

"Yes, ma'am. I invited her to come meet Shriver."

Birdie's eyes widened. She threw her head back with open-mouthed giggles. "Lois, this poor girl doesn't want to spend all her time doing *something useful!*"

Lois stood and dusted off her dress, her shoulders jumping with suppressed laughter. "You stop! I think it's a good match." She turned to Grammie. "We just love irking his nerves, that's all, Libby dear. He throws such fits. But his bark is worse than his bite. This is Birdie. We're soon to be sisters."

"It's nice to meet you," Grammie said.

"There's no use being bashful around here, doll," Lois said, marching passed little Evie and almost kicking her. She flung an arm around Grammie. "I'm sorry I didn't tell you the real reason why I invited you. *But* Shriver is handsome, isn't he? Maybe you can soften him up a bit."

Lois began to pull Grammie away from the patch, and Birdie ran to catch up. Before they had walked very far, both apparitions vanished like smoke dissipating into the air and leaving the old woman standing alone. Grammie glanced around bewildered. Evie didn't waste a moment to rush over and take her hand.

"Why…I don't know…" Grammie was saying.

"It's okay, Grammie. We were just going to the garden," Evie offered.

"The garden?"

"Yes."

"Evie… Did you know, the first time I came to this place, your Pappy lived in a house that used to be right there, through those trees…"

"You told me, Grammie."

"I did?"

"Lots of times. Remember? Let's go to the garden."

"The garden."

"Yes."

"Through the path between the wood…"

Now Evie was certain that she had not seen ghosts because Aunt Lois was very much alive. Aunt Lois had grown old, but there was no doubt the young Lois had been her, just as Grammie must have remembered her from long ago. Children catch on to things very quickly, you see.

The next part of this story takes place back at Grammie's house, and it was added later by Lawrence Newbell. Evie didn't know this part for some years, but it was not necessary. She already knew the stories Aunt Lois told. This part is included for the reader.

Back at Grammie's house, Lawrence and Jen Newbell had taken a break from their task. Jen stretched her back and gathered her things to leave, for her brother was no longer focused. He had found old photographs, and she knew what that meant. He would be engrossed for hours.

"Have you ever seen these before?" he asked her.

She rolled her eyes. "Probably, but hey, I'm gonna go. I still need to get my casserole in the oven for tonight."

Lawrence only half heard her. He held a worn, black and white photograph. Two young people smiled at the camera. He had never known his parents when they looked like they did there. Baldy Newbell was a head taller than his young bride. He was the picture of robust health. She was like a dainty flower crushed against his side. A gentle stream and thick forest made the background behind them.

"Hey, wait," Lawrence said.

Jen put her hands on her hips.

"Just look at this picture of Mom and Dad. I never saw them this happy."

Jen took the photograph from his hand, then grinned. "Oh *my*, that's *the* spot."

"*The* spot?"

"Tell me you don't remember," she derided him.

He gave an exasperated sigh.

"I just *can't* believe you don't remember this," she said. But she took a briefer moment than usual to revel in knowing something that her brother did not. "Alright. Maybe Mom didn't bother you with this since you were a boy." She leaned against the back of a kitchen chair and folded her arms. "So, you know how superstitious Aunt Lois is. Well, Mom was younger than all of them, and she was the only one who wasn't married yet. The only eligible bachelor in Lois' family was of course Dad. So, Aunt Lois told Mom that there was a flower called St. John's Wort that can supposedly tell who a girl will marry." She paused for dramatic effect. "Do you see where this is going?"

He did. "St. John's *wort*?"

"Yes, well, *you* don't call it that. It's goat's weed."

Lawrence stared at her. "You're kidding. You mean that devilish stuff that won't cut and doesn't ever die and stains everything?"

She laughed. "That's the stuff."

"Mom fell for *that*?"

"Would you just listen? I guess down around the little path behind the garden where we used to take the four-wheelers through is where it used to grow. Aunt Lois told Mom that if you crush the plant so that there is blood on both of your hands, the next man you see is to be your husband."

"*Blood*?"

"The red stuff it secretes."

He sighed. "I *know* what you mean. That's the most ridiculous thing I've ever heard."

"Well, so you know what happened. Mom did it, looked up, and there was Dad. Ta-da!"

Lawrence laughed thinking of his father. "I bet he was happy to know his fate was up to goat's weed."

"Yeah, seriously."

"So, did Aunt Lois send him there for Mom?"

Jen shrugged. "You know Aunt Lois. But who knows? Maybe it's true."

"*Yeah.*"

She waved her finger at him. "Now, now, Mr. Practical! Maybe magic can be real when you're open to it." She took her keys from her purse. "But hey, I really gotta go. I'll see you later."

Lawrence nodded a goodbye in her direction and turned his attention back to the photographs.

Evie's story returns now to the way she told it, on the path between the wood.

Their feet padded on the forest bed. Evie could hear the trickling of water from the nearby stream just out of view. The path led to an open glen where the large garden had always been planted. No sprouting green plants or sunflowers would be there now. In times past, the pumpkins, squash, zucchinis, tomatoes and watermelons produced were some of the biggest the community ever saw. There had been no planting on the Newbell property after Pappy's death.

Grammie walked behind Evie. Her knees cracked. She stretched out her fingers and twisted her tightening wrists. They were following a trail that felt familiar to her, where yellow wildflowers that were as tall as her once grew. When Grammie's eyes caught sight of them again, she stopped walking.

Evie heard Grammie stop. She turned back in time to see the mist return to Grammie's eyes, and now tall bushes topped with yellow blossoms stood next to them that had not been there a moment ago.

Grammie stared into the palms of her hands for what seemed like a long time and then gingerly touched the tip of one yellow petal. Evie tilted her head to the side as she watched. The old woman pulled off the blossom and rubbed it vigorously between both palms. Evie was not confused, though. She remembered the story Aunt Lois told.

In the stillness, Evie now heard footsteps crunching through the wood. Grammie heard them too and stared into the trees. They grew louder and closer until suddenly a man emerged onto the path where they stood. It was Shriver, and he didn't see them.

Grammie's misty eyes seemed to brighten, and her pasty cheeks flushed. Shriver was looking down, and the rim of the ballcap he now wore covered his eyes from view. Suddenly, Evie realized he still had not yet seen Grammie, but before she could call out a warning, he plowed right into her.

Shriver jumped back with surprise and gaped at Grammie.

"Oh, hello, Shriver," Grammie said after a moment, her lips curving into a shy smile.

He balked. "Hello."

Evie glanced from one to the other.

"We're having a picnic," he said at last.

"Yes. Lois invited me."

"Of course, she did," he muttered.

"So, I'll see you there?"

"Yep." He pushed passed Grammie and stalked off into the wood without looking back. The sound of his footsteps faded instantly, but Grammie's gaze lingered after him. Evie waited for the mist to disappear, but this time it didn't.

Finally, Grammie noticed her, but her eyes did not light up.

Grammie clasped her hands together. "Why, what's your name, little girl?"

Evie stood very still. She twisted the fabric of her skirt in her hands wondering what to do. At last, she said, "I'm Evie."

"Where are you off to, Evie?"

She thought for a minute and smiled. "To the picnic."

"Really? I'm headed there myself. We can go together."

Hand in hand, they walked back to Grammie' house, but the yard looked much different than when they had left it. It was a richer green, and the apple tree sprouted lush fruit. There was a redbrick house next to the strawberry patch with picnic tables lined up in the front yard. Red and white checkered table cloths flapped in the breeze, and food platters sent a mouthwatering aroma into the air.

All at once, images of people burst into view. Their voices hit Evie's ears. The women all wore floral dresses and scampered about fussing over food and children. The men congregated by shining pick-up trucks of the likes Evie had never seen and never would see in her day. Children ran laughing and squealing through the yard.

Evie recognized Lois calling above the noise. "Spook!"

A burly man with a square jaw looked over at her but said nothing.

"Harvey Elmer Newbell, I'm talking to you!"

"What is it?"

"Where is our son?"

In answer to her question, the girl with two long braids, who had been by the fish pond earlier, came bounding around the corner of the house. "Mama, he's playing on Grandpap's tractor again!"

Lois groaned. "Albert," she called, beginning her pursuit, "Come here boy!"

Albert rounded the corner of the house, but Shriver, still wearing the ballcap, suddenly appeared to scoop up the running child before Lois could get to him. The pair fell to the ground together in a fit of laughter. Shiver's hat flew off to reveal a freshly shaved head.

"Hey, look at Shriver!" said Spook. "What did you go and shave off all your hair for? The war's over!"

Another man added, "Hey *Baldy*!"

Evie and Grammie stood at the bottom of the hill away from the activity and watched for a long time.

When they returned to the house later, Daddy had pushed the paperwork aside and spread the old photographs across the table instead.

"Mom," he said without looking up, "I don't remember all these."

Grammie patted him on the shoulder. "So many memories," she said. Her voice was weak and breathless. "I'm not feeling so well. I'm going to lie down and take a rest." She stopped in the doorway of the hall. "If you two leave before I wake up, thank you for visiting. It was a good day."

They weren't leaving. They planned to take her the picnic at Aunt Lois' later, but neither one reminded her. They would wake her later.

"Goodnight, Grammie," said Evie.

Daddy reached for Evie and pulled her onto his lap. He heard the sound of his mother's bedroom door clicking shut down the hall.

"Evie, look here."

Evie secretly slipped her thumb into her mouth. Daddy showed her photograph after photograph, but she had seen all of these people just moments ago.

"…and this is Uncle Harvey. Great Uncle Harvey to you," Daddy said.

"Spook," she said around her thumb.

"What? Did I tell you that?" But Daddy didn't stop to wonder how she knew the nickname. "And here is a picture of your Aunt Lois and my cousins."

Behind them, the front door opened with hardly a sound. Evie turned, but Daddy did not notice. He kept talking and picking through photographs. But that is not why he didn't hear or see Pappy walk into the house. Only little children see spirits of heaven most of the time.

With her thumb still in her mouth, Evie grinned at Pappy. Perhaps she would not have recognized him if she had not seen Grammie's memories. This was not the feeble, grumpy, old man who could barely support her on his lap. This was young Shriver with sparkling eyes. His smile was warm and radiant, and his skin seemed to glow. He reached over, tweaked her nose and winked. Then he put a finger to his lips.

She watched him disappear down the hall. He seemed to glide.

"This is the yard right out here," Daddy was saying, holding up a photograph of children kicking around a ball in the grass. "They used to have the Newbell family reunion here, but the family got too big, and we moved it to the park." He picked up another one. "Do you know who this is?"

Evie studied the face of the little boy. It was a color photograph and not as old as the rest. The boy had brown eyes like hers. She took her thumb out of her mouth long enough to say, "It's you, Daddy."

"That's right. I was about your age. That's me in kindergarten."

Soon, Pappy came back down the hall. He guided the young woman from the mirror behind him. They paused next to Evie, and the lovely woman leaned down. She whispered, "What did I tell you about that?" She gently pulled Evie's thumb out of her mouth. It made a kissing sound. The woman smiled. "You take good care of your Daddy."

Pappy quietly opened the front door and ushered Grammie out. He winked again at Evie and shut the door behind them. Evie wiggled away from Daddy and slid to the floor. She hurried to the door herself and turned the handle with both hands to open it.

"Where are you going?" Daddy asked her without looking up.

Pappy and Grammie stood across the front yard near the roadside. They looked back and saw Evie. Grammie knelt down with her arms outstretched.

Lawrence said later that he went to the door to check on Evie after she went running from the house. He saw her laughing and spinning around and around in the yard. As he watched, his heart must have begun to beat like that of a child, at least for just a moment, because he almost thought he saw the silhouettes of a young man and woman dancing with her.

Pappy spun Evie around one last time. She giggled with dizziness. Then he took Grammie into his arms. They looked into one another's eyes and began to rise above the ground. Evie watched them slowly vanish into the sunlight. That was the part of the story that made Elizabeth Newbell's passing in her sleep that day much easier on the family members who believed Evie's story.

When the couple had gone, Evie noticed for the first time that a few of the tall, yellow wildflowers were growing by the side of the road. She had never seen them there before. They were shorter than the ones Grammie had seen earlier. She approached them cautiously, wondering if it was wise to play with magic. But Evie was only five years old. She narrowed her eyes and touched one blossom with tender fingers. Little black dots speckled the yellow. She pinched it, producing a tiny bit of dark stain on her index finger and thumb. She rubbed her hands together, smudging the stain into her skin.

That's when Hugh Thomas, the seven-year-old who had just moved in down the lane with his parents, stepped on a stick behind the nearest pine tree and gave away his presence. Evie's eyes darted to him and caught his gaze. Golden strands of hair blew across her face. Hugh shoved his hands into his blue jean pockets and stared back for a moment before blushing and darting away.

For years, Evie and Hugh rarely saw each other except from a distance, when Evie's family visited the mountain house to prepare it to sell. They never spoke to each other until the graduated middle-schoolers from both the mountains and the valley met for the first time at the high school in the tenth grade. Hugh was surprised to be so drawn to a girl, but Evie had been expecting it.

Well, what do you think?

In memory of Gramma and Pap.

WATCHER OF CEMETERY LANE

The German name for the chicory plant is 'watcher of the road.'
According to a German legend, a young girl once waited every day
along the roadside for her lover. When he never returned, she died of a
broken heart. The blue chicory grew up from where she died.

The dog appeared on the side of the road as Jude rounded the
bend. He saw it just in time to screech to a stop in his old pickup.
The animal looked into his eyes. It was a black Labrador. Shiny
and young.

"Well, go on, boy," Jude said under his breath.

Finally, the dog padded across the road and disappeared into
the trees. Jude wondered where it was going. He had never seen it
before. Must be new. He would have to keep an eye out.

The pickup truck lumbered on down the road. Jude chanced a
glance in the rearview mirror. He could see the dip where the road
had intersected with Cemetery Lane. He braced himself against
the pang in his chest, but it was too late. His heart spasmed.

What were the chances of the dog stopping him right there? Jude had avoided even looking at Cemetery Lane since last June.

He took a deep breath and shook it off. He just had to get through the summer. He'd always known it would hurt the most in the summer. After the winter melted away and the leaves came back, every day reminded him of Mary. Some mornings, he would wake to the rooster and sunshine and think it really had been just a bad dream. Like last summer had come back to give him a second chance instead of haunting him like a ghost.

Jude turned the pickup onto his own lane. The chickens were too close to the road again. When was the last time he had given them anything to eat? Come to think of it, he needed to eat, too. Eating was such a depressing thing.

Mary had rarely invited him for dinner, but she had asked him over several times those last few weeks. Maybe if he had showed up more often, got to the fence mending when she asked, or something, she would have softened sooner. Then again, he thought she might have warmed to him on account of him not pressing her so much.

Mary was a challenge, that was for sure. But for all his life, he had loved only her. That was the way it had always been, and it was the way it would stay.

Jude parked next to the house. The wind blew in waves across the grass. He would have to mow soon. No, he might as well do it now. It would be dark when he was done, but sometimes he liked it that way.

A few hours later, Jude eased the tractor back into the lower garage. He shut off the engine, but a low grumbling continued.

Oh. His stomach. He had forgotten about that. This time, he really was ready to eat. What would it be? Peanut butter bread and pickles again? Eggs, too, probably. There was always eggs. Eating was such a depressing thing.

The moon tonight was a low, silver bulb brightening the cloud-less sky with its ever-cool light. Jude could see as far in the moon-light as he could in the sunshine. Maybe farther, since the light didn't hurt his eyes. He never minded the night, especially out-doors. He found it peaceful, like a dreamland.

When he was halfway back to the house, a dog's bark stung the air. He stopped. The neighbors who had dogs didn't live that close. Could it be the same animal as earlier? Maybe it was lost after all.

He hesitated. His stomach rumbled again.

Well, the night was so bright. He might be able to help. Then again, the dog had gone off in the direction of Cemetery Lane. He definitely wasn't going there, but he supposed he could walk just far enough until he would be able to see Cemetery Lane if he went any further. If the dog was beyond that point, it was out of luck.

It had never occurred to Jude until last summer that Cemetery Lane was a poor name for a road. He despised it. He couldn't look at the street sign, either. He had not been down Cemetery Lane since he'd helped clean out Mary's things. He couldn't look at the gravestones across the lane from her house. He couldn't look at her house itself. He could only look at the few photographs he had. Mary wasn't much for taking pictures, but he'd coerced her into some. He would remember everything the way it had been. The memories were all he had now.

His boots thudded on the pavement. "Here, boy," he called softly and clicked his tongue.

From a distance came a soft whine.

He called a bit louder. "Come, boy."

The dog barked. One sharp yip, like an answer. Jude increased his stride. At last, he saw a dark mass along the side of the road. Two eyes glinted in the moonlight.

'There ya are, boy. What's-the-matter?" He clicked his tongue, slowing his step. "Ya, alright?"

Jude cautiously closed the gap between them. The dog was sitting up. A low, barely audible whine floated from it.

"I'm not gonna hurt ya. It's alright."

When he had almost reached the dog, it stood. It met his gaze just as it had earlier. But something made him stop. The dog stared at him. It didn't appear hurt. It turned and trotted a few paces away and glanced back.

"I can't go that way," Jude said. "If you want my help, you've gotta come with me."

The dog considered him, but it left anyway, rounding the bend that would bring it to Cemetery Lane.

Jude stayed in place. There was something about the dog that felt familiar. Like it could understand what he said.

And it had nothing to say back. It had called for him, made him believe he was needed, only to reject him when he came too close.

He shook his head. Mary had said she never wanted to get married. She had said it, but he just knew she would change her mind. Life was hard alone. He was always there for her. He made sure she always knew. In the end, she would have opened up to him, he was sure of it.

Except that's not what had happened. In the end, he was not there for her when she needed him most of all.

Jude's heart spasmed again. He clutched his chest. He took a deep, shuddering breath, turned on his heel and went home.

The next morning when he left for work, he remembered the dog and drove down the road slowly, watching the woods for any sign of it.

An all too familiar twinge scampered up his chest as he rounded the bend. He averted his eyes like always, but this time, his gaze was drawn back by a flash of blue. There, along the side of the road, a few yards before the intersection of Cemetery Lane, stood a chicory plant.

Jude rolled passed it, craning his neck to look at it like he was waiting for it to act like a human, too. The dog had been near here. Actually, he thought this was the very spot. A chill passed through him.

So, it was time for the chicory. He had half-forgotten it until now. Chicory had been all over the forest when they searched for Mary. It was her favorite wildflower. Blue like her eyes. They had spread out in a line just like in the movies.

"Mary!" Everyone's voices calling from their allotted sector. The police with their dogs.

The neighbor Rebecca was the one that had first noticed Mary missing. Jude hated that it wasn't him. Mary had said she would mill flour that day. Rebecca was to buy a bag.

It wasn't as simple as Mary just being *out* though. Mary was never "out." Outside, yes. The woman never stopped working. But she rarely left the farm. She did her errands on Saturdays, church on Sundays, and that was about it. It had been that way ever since her father died. She was only seventeen years old when he passed. So was Jude.

The loss of Mary's father had changed her, but not much. She was always private. Jude remembered the first time he tried to spend time with her in a way that wasn't about the land.

"You know, I was thinking, Mary," he said. "I don't have to pick Ma up for church anymore. I could take you… if you wanted."

He watched her eyes flutter away. "I don't mind driving," she said.

"I know. It's just, you live right here. There's no reason for us both to-"

"I like driving myself."

Heat rushed to his cheeks. He was glad she wasn't looking at him. "That's alright. I was just saying. If you change your mind, you can just-"

"I won't change my mind." Her voice was sweet but stern.

The next thing he knew, they were comparing models of tractors again. He didn't mind what they talked about, as long as she was talking to him.

Jude had thought maybe Mary was annoyed with men asking her for a date. To others, she was a beautiful mystery. They wanted to crack her.

Jude knew there was no mystery. Not to him. She just knew what she wanted in life, and she didn't have to explain it to anybody. Just like she said she would never marry.

It wasn't that he wanted to change her. He would never want that. He just knew Mary and him were the same. They had practically lived on the same land their whole lives. They knew each other the way they knew that land. They were all connected. Jude, Mary, and the old Ryan farm that was now split up between all the folks on the ridge. Two people that belonged to that land belonged with each other.

And nothing had changed even now. He and Mary were both still part of the land, and he was still separated from her.

At first, they had all thought Mary might be hurt. No one thought she was dead. When the second night passed, Jude knew they were looking for more than Mary. They were looking for evidence of what might have killed her. Wild animals, to be specific.

He couldn't think about that though. They searched for days. When the search was given up, he kept looking alone. Even after her memorial service, he couldn't stop.

What if she was cold and alone? Even if she was gone, how could he just leave her out there? She needed him. He knew her better than anyone. Why couldn't he find her?

The reverend had patted him on the shoulder one Sunday after service.

"I know you loved her, son," he said softly. "Mary knew it, too. You did well looking after her all these years. Her father would be grateful. Your Ma would be proud, too. You can let go of Mary, when you're ready, because you did right by her all the way to the end. And where she is, she knows that, too."

So, he had stopped looking. He stopped looking at anything down Cemetery Lane at all.

But the chicory was back now, just like when they first combed the forest. Did it still hide her beneath it now like it had then?

Work was grueling that day. Jude couldn't focus. He almost took his finger off with the metal lathe. And he almost didn't see the dog along the road when he passed Cemetery Lane on his way back home again.

The dog came into view at the intersection. For the second time, Jude slammed on his brakes at the same spot. The dog slinked away from the truck and vanished into the trees.

Jude caught his breath. "Hey, wait a minute!" He shot out of the cab. "Come here!" He clicked his tongue loudly. Against his better judgment, he even went into the forest. But the dog was nowhere to be seen. Far ahead, he recognized more chicory flowers in bloom.

Jude grabbed for his heart just as the pang shot through it. Mary couldn't be trying to tell him something, could she?

He scrubbed his hands over his face. He had no interest in finding Mary now. She was preserved safe in his memory the way he wanted her to stay. He couldn't bear for that image to change.

"Go home, dog! Leave me alone!" he shouted. He had to get a grip.

That night, Jude sat on the porch with a beer in spite of himself. He told himself he wouldn't go if he heard the dog bark, but he couldn't bring himself not to listen for it anyway.

The night was full of stars. They twinkled like the fireflies that filled the forest across the street. Crickets chirped, but there was nothing else.

If you give me a second chance, he had prayed the same prayer so often last year. *I won't let anything happen to her this time. I just need a second chance.*

He had prayed so much as he traipsed through the forest. The blue chicory bloomed all around as though it was springing up from his tear drops.

A second chance. How often had he opened his eyes in the morning willing the day to be just that? But it never came. If he couldn't save Mary for real, he would at least keep her safe in his heart.

You can let go of Mary, when you're ready.

"Why would I ever be ready for that?" he asked aloud.

Because you did right by her all the way to the end.

He thought about the dog and the times he had seen it. It was always in the same area.

He glanced up at the stars. "Lord, if you are trying to tell me something, I'm going to need strength."

He downed the last of his beer and pushed himself off the porch. He would at least check.

Jude's heart raced, but he walked down the road faster to keep up with it. If there was no dog, he was only fooling himself. If there was a dog, well, he would do right by Mary, whatever it meant.

He knew the dog was there long before he neared it. He could make out the black figure sitting as still as a rock. As he came upon it, the moonlight revealed the chicory plant posted beside it like a partner in crime. Or was it somehow part of the dog itself? The whole thing was so bizarre.

"What're you doing here, boy?" he murmured.

The dog opened its mouth in a pant. It stood up and inched toward him. He held out a hand and allowed a long, wet sniff. Then he patted the top of its head. At least the dog was real. When he reached for it again, it shied away.

"Now, now, none of that. What's the deal, eh?"

Jude took a small step forward. When the dog didn't move, he slowly began to pat it again. It seemed to finally be warming to him.

"Well, my apologies, ma'am. I didn't know," he said.

The dog was a girl. He felt trepidation rise within him. He had been hoping he was making it all up. Did this dog really mean to lead him to Mary? Was this somehow, in some way, Mary?

All at once, an owl screeched somewhere in the trees. When he flinched, the dog jerked away and darted into the forest. Into the darkness.

"Wait!" he called, but he could hear it moving farther and farther away.

"I'll come, Mary," he vowed. Next time, he wouldn't let her out of his sight.

The next time Jude heard the dog bark, he was replacing the mower blades in the garage. This time, the sound was like an alarm. Something was wrong. He couldn't shove his tools aside fast enough. He hadn't seen or heard the dog in days. He had almost decided he was crazy after all.

He flung his hat down and ran faster than he had in years. The sun was high in the sky. It baked down on him in his heavy jeans and boots. Almost right away, his lungs felt like fire.

At the bend in the road, he saw something moving fast through the trees. The dog was running through the forest toward the road. They reached one another at the same time. The dog barked again and again in alarm, turning around in circles.

"Alright, girl," he said, taking steps to her to show her he would follow. "Show me. Go on."

She met his eyes, yipped, and darted back the way she had come. Jude ran after her down into the forest. He tried not to let his mind go. Part of him still didn't want to know where the dog would take him. Something inside told him there would be no going back. But he had to, for Mary.

They tore through green brush and briers that were nearly full again. He felt tiny jaggers yanking and scratching at his jeans. His legs pushed through the shrubs, no doubt uprooting anything that clung to him. Ahead, the dog bounded across the forest bed unscathed.

"Wait up!" he called. As though she understood, the dog stopped and waited, pacing and whining until he caught up. Then off she went again.

It took all his strength to keep up. He felt he might be faltering. The dog's barks echoed through the trees, and the memories Jude had been trying to hold back came flooding into his mind.

He envisioned the other canines charging through the forest followed by police officers. He had stayed close to the dogs. They were most likely to find her first. Now here he was chasing a dog again through the same trees. The forest felt bigger this time. Everything looked down at him, taunting him. He noticed the chicory. He was surrounded by it as though it had all started blooming the moment he stepped foot into the forest.

All the vegetation was heavy. Everything was awakened with life now like it had been a year ago. The forest was speckled with wildflowers of every color, but none so dazzling as the blue chicory. What Mary had once thought so beautiful had cruelly hid the most beautiful thing of all.

His heart pounded like it would burst through his chest. His legs felt heavy as stone, but still he pushed on.

Lord, I need you. If this is my second chance, help me save her. Let me find her this time.

He had no idea where he was, but he knew they had gone in a direction parallel to Cemetery Lane. He wondered how they had not come upon Mary's small farm yet.

The incline was getting steeper. He could hardly keep up with his legs running downhill. The momentum was all that kept him from stumbling.

At the bottom, a creek sliced across the forest, separating him from the other side. The dog didn't stop. She leaped across it with no hesitation. Jude knew that would never happen for him. He didn't even try. He just splashed down through the water and climbed back up the opposite bank.

"Where are you?" he called.

The dog answered with barking. He gasped for breath and charged in her direction.

"I don't see you!"

The farther he went, the louder the barking became. *She's stopped*, he realized.

Jude slowed down. Was this it? He tried to brace himself.

The creek had snaked around again to where the dog now stood along the bank. When she saw Jude approach, she barked right at him.

"I'm coming," he whispered.

He scanned the forest bed as he made his way to the dog. The chicory buds stared back at him like hundreds of blue-eyed sentinels. He saw nothing that he was looking for, not that he knew for sure what that was, until he stood next to the dog.

There, half fallen into the tinkling water and half embraced by a bed of chicory was a woman. She was face down, her upper body atop the rocks of the stream and her brown hair surrounding her head like a veil that concealed a secret.

His heart jerked so hard he thought it stopped.

Mary...?

The dog nudged the unmoving woman.

Jude's prayers burst into his mind. Had the Lord really brought her back? Was this that kind of second chance? In his desperation, he had dared to hope.

In a flash, he was down in the water. With trembling fingers, he brushed her hair aside. There was blood on the rock beneath her head. His breath caught.

Was she... gone?

No, he could feel her warm beneath his hand. Gently, he pulled the woman into his arms, turning her around. This time, when he brushed her hair from her face, his heart fell.

He closed his eyes and forced a breath. He tried to brace himself against the shock, the confusion, and the wall of pain. It all fell upon him anyway.

The woman was not Mary.

The cold nose of the dog pressed into his arm. He shook himself and looked into the deep, pleading gaze of the animal inches from his face. It imparted some strength to him. "I got her," he said. For the first time, he looked over the woman's wounds. Just some scratches on her arms, face and neck. It was the laceration on her forehead that was the problem. She probably slipped and fell. "I got her."

The dog led the way through the forest. Jude carried the woman, following the dog with the same blind trust that had brought him to her in the first place.

Later, at the hospital, Jude stood around uncomfortably. He had left the dog on his farm and followed the ambulance. What would he even say to the woman when she woke up? Would she even want to speak to a stranger? He was no hero anyway. It was her amazing dog that had rescued her. He supposed he could at least tell her that. She would want to know.

"You can go back now, sir," the nurse said.

He took a deep breath. If she was anything like Mary, she wouldn't be one for talking anyway.

When he stepped into the small hospital room, the woman was awake and sitting up in the bed with a bandaged forehead. Their eyes met, and she smiled at once. Jude stopped short.

"Hi! You're Jude?"

His heart did a little spasm, but not the same as before. He nodded.

Her eyes flickered to his chest. He glanced down and saw the blood. "Oh, don't worry about that," he said. "I'm glad you're okay."

"I am. Thanks to you."

He felt heat rise to his face, and unfortunately, this woman was still staring right at him. He cleared his throat and turned away himself. "Not really."

"I was knocked unconscious in a stream." She giggled. "I have a concussion. I'm pretty sure things were bad for me until you came along. How did you find me?"

"Your dog," he said quickly. "She led me to you. And she's fine. I left her at my place with some food. I live down the road."

"Really? Watcher did that? Huh."

He ventured a glance. "She came and got me. I followed her right to you. It was amazing. You seem surprised?"

She shrugged. "Well, yeah. I just got her. I'm not sure if she found me or I found her. I guess I don't know her that well yet. I'm Andrea, by the way. I moved into the Turner house. I'm a cousin. You can sit down, if you want."

Jude sat in the only chair available, right beside her bed. She looked pretty even with the bandage. She had wide eyes that sparkled like emeralds.

"I've never seen you before," he said. The Turners owned property at the end of Cemetery Lane. He knew all the Turners.

She laughed. "Everybody knows everybody around here. I'm learning that. I'm not from here, obviously. I just needed a fresh start. My uncle had the house."

"You're by yourself?"

Her smile faltered.

"Oh-" He fumbled for words. "I…I didn't mean it like that. I just mean, I guess, what were you doing in the woods alone like that?"

She laughed again. "I might have got carried away. I was exploring. Looking for what kind of berries and things are out there. I really don't know what I'm doing yet. I've never lived in the country before."

A strand of her loose hair fell down in her face. She casually tucked it behind her ear. She seemed so at ease and open, even with him.

"So, are *you* alone?" she asked. Her gaze captured his.

"Yeah. I… yeah." He dropped his head slightly.

"I hear you. It's not so bad sometimes. It's hard to get used to though. For me anyway."

"I don't think I'll ever get used to it," he found himself saying. "But it is what it is."

She narrowed her eyes.

"So, the dog's name is Watcher?" he asked.

"Mm-hmm. Well, I don't know her name, but that's what I decided to call her. She's always going out and waiting by the road. That's where I found her. It's like she's watching for someone to come back every night. I think she might have lost someone, too. No one's ever claimed her though, so she's mine now. I think everything like that happens for a reason, you know? Like you finding me today. We may never understand why there was pain and sadness in our lives, but hope always comes again if we let it. I'm hoping this is a second chance for Watcher and me. I think we both need it."

I just need a second chance…

She caught him staring and smiled. "You know what? You should come for dinner sometime."

He swallowed. "D-dinner?"

"Sure," she said, somewhat shyly. "I can thank you properly for saving me. Besides, it'd be nice to cook for someone else. What do you think?"

Hope always comes again if we let it.

You can let go of Mary, when you're ready.

He felt his lips start to tip on their own, and somehow, he decided to let them. Finally, he said, "I really don't like eating alone."

LEGEND OF THE
WOLF CHILD

*Ancient Germans used a purple wildflower to poison wolves, giving it
the name wolfbane. It was believed to be used to reverse shape shifting
spells and has a folk tradition attached to it of protecting homes against
werewolves. Witches were thought to dip flints in the juice of wolfbane
to create weapons to throw at enemies. One scratch was enough to kill.
Ingesting even a tiny amount of this plant can be fatal.*

*The following letter was found on the desk of Dr. Jesse Talbot ensu-
ing his fatal illness, addressed to no one in particular but assumed to
be meant for his children. Until now, the Talbot family withheld the
document from publication with Dr. Talbot's other papers. It came
to me not as editor of the Botanical Gazette, for it was not intend-
ed for publication. It was requested by the heirs that the document
remain at the college for the reason that it was the last writing of a
distinguished botanist. When I recognized the value of the long and
personal letter, I convinced the heirs to allow it to be published. They
consented on the condition that it was not done until all family mem-*

bers who had been alive during the documented events were deceased. For a reason that I am wholly at a loss to understand, that has only now become the case.

Columbia College, New York City, 1961

1. THE WEREWOLF

THERE IS A legend you may know. It is said that there once lived a farmer and his wife in Idaho. They had no children of their own. One day while hunting in the mountains, the farmer discovered a feral girl living among a pack of American Gray Wolves. He managed to bring the girl home, but she only resented her captors. In time, the girl ran away, but her wolf pack had moved on. According to the legend, the girl stayed in the mountains searching and waiting, and she is still there to this day. When the people of Clearwater County hear a lone wolf's howl in the night, they say it is the wolf child calling in vain for her long-lost family.

In honor of my parent's wishes, I, too, allowed this story to prevail. I have even been amused that I was left out of it. But now that I am old, I must tell you what really happened, supposing she ever does come home again.

To begin, we lived in a rural community, Mama, Pa and I. Our valley was hugged by the Bitteroot Mountain Range not far from the Montana border. I was the firstborn son and only child of Abraham and Fee Talbot, born with the destiny to work our farm alongside my father. In those days, folk traditions regulated the people's lives, all but Pa's. I had only ever heard of and not seen a wolf, let alone a werewolf, but I knew fantastical stories about both.

One day in the late autumn when I was seven years old, I heard Mama scream. When I ran around the corner of the barn, I saw a brown wolf dashing away from her. Mama was crumbled on the ground. Pa fired a shot at it but missed. From the tree line, the animal glanced back at us. A jagged scar trailed down the left side of its face from eye to throat. Then just like that, it vanished into the wood.

Mama's arm was covered in blood.

"Fill the dish tub," Pa barked to me as he lifted her.

I hurried ahead of them into the house. Pa put Mama on the kitchen bench, and I handed him a clean sponge. Red water soon soaked my mother's gingham apron as Pa washed her arm. He pressed her thin muscles at the wound until the bleeding stopped.

"A needle and thread," he said.

I retrieved the items and watched him stitch and dab. Mama bit her lip. The needle hooked her delicate skin and pulled it tight, but she didn't make a sound. When the awful thing was done, Pa dressed the wound with cloths.

Mama finally pulled me into her embrace. "Don't be frightened," she said. She smelled of her powder, but it was mixed with the copper scent of blood and the waxy, mineral fraught medicine Pa had put on the bite.

"Why did the wolf do it?" I asked her.

Pa had always told me wolves were not dangerous to people. Even hungry wolves did not attack humans. They only attacked weak animals in the forest, and I needn't be afraid when I heard them howling in the nights.

Mama kissed my hair, but Pa interjected, "If a wild animal

comes close like that, shoot it. It's probably sick."

Pa decided he would take Mama to the doctor in town, and I would stay at the house with the rifle to keep watch. I did not like the plan much, but I didn't tell Pa. Though I wanted the wolf dead as much as anybody, I didn't want to see it again. The animal was callous and cold and not in the least afraid of Pa's shooting at it.

Pa and Mama returned at dusk. When it didn't seem they were going to tell me anything, I asked Mama what the doctor had said.

She offered a fragile smile. "He said I will heal, Jesse."

"But was the wolf sick?"

She glanced above my head at Pa. I felt his presence go rigid behind me. "The wolf was not sick it seems," she said.

That night, Mama sat in the rocking chair near the window instead of her usual seat by the fire, where she took up her knitting.

I crawled into her lap even though Pa had said I was too old for it. "Why are you and Pa sad?" I whispered.

"We're only tired," she whispered back.

I shook my head. "Pa is more than tired."

She sighed and started rocking. "Don't you worry about your Pa. He just loves us, and he's concerned. Sometimes learning how to love the best takes the longest time, but people are always learning new things. I think there's a bit of magic in the world that teaches us, and we don't even notice it's happening. But it is."

It didn't seem to me Pa ever learned something new. He knew how to do everything already, and he had his way of doing it, and to him, it was already the best.

"Pa says there's no such thing as–"

"Oh, I think there is," she said. "I think magic and love and are made of the same thing."

Over the next few days, Mama's arm healed, and our lives went back to normal. But Mama and Pa were much quieter. Every night, Mama still sat in the rocking chair by the window. One night, I went to her again.

"What do you keep looking for at night?" I asked. I hoped she would confide in me if Pa didn't hear. "Are you afraid the wolf will come back?"

She rested her head against the back of the chair. "I'm just looking at the moon. It will be full tomorrow. It's pretty, don't you think?"

The cold, white body was large as the window. It felt foreboding. Before I could reply, Mama pulled my face into her shoulder, cradling me tight.

As I remember it now, I started recalling the stories of men changing into wolves at the time of a full moon, but those thoughts left me quickly. They were tall tales. Pa always hated when I believed tall tales that kept me awake at night. He wanted me to be brave and strong. I was neither yet, but I tried my best to please him and to hide it when I felt afraid. Many times, I would lay awake in my bed listening to the night sounds. A far-off screech owl sounding like screaming. Footfalls in the wood. A stirring in the yard. I imagined many demons of the forest come to wreak havoc on the farm while they could be cloaked in darkness. Pa hated those tales. I did, too, but I believed them.

The next night, after we had gone to bed, Pa suddenly burst into my room.

"Where is she?" His voice boomed. He knocked into my bed in the shadows. Then he went back out and down the stairs. He crashed through the house calling Mama's name. The front door opened and slammed shut. I heard his heavy footsteps hurry across the porch.

I ran down the stairs and out the door. Out in the darkness, I heard him say Mama's name like he had found her, but something was wrong.

I rushed across the dewy earth to his side expecting to see Mama crumpled on the ground again. Instead, there stood a small, white wolf peering at us in the shadows. I gasped and turned to run, but Pa grabbed me.

"Fee," he said through a breath.

I watched in awed terror as the white wolf padded into the moonshine. I struggled to get out of Pa's grip, but he still held me fast.

"It's-it's a wolf, Pa!"

The creature crept closer. It glided right up to us. A warm, velvety tongue shot out of it's mouth and licked my hand.

"Don't move," Pa whispered.

I didn't, but just as the brown wolf had left us without another thought, the white wolf turned and darted through the yard. It disappeared into the wood in a flash.

"No!" Pa let me go and ran after it calling Mama's name. I stood trembling until he came back and pushed past me. I went inside after him and ran to Mama and Pa's bedroom.

Mama wasn't there.

I rushed through the house searching in the darkness as Pa had done. She wasn't anywhere.

Pa was standing by the window. When I finally went to him, I was met by his grim face cast aglow in the moonlight.

"You know what happened," he said. "We'll have to wait for the daylight to go after her."

The stories burst into my mind. I had known the brown wolf was different. It wasn't afraid. And Mama's wounds had healed quickly. Mama had been waiting for something as she watched the phases of the autumn moon. I thought I knew the truth the moment the white wolf looked at me. She was the most beautiful creature I had ever seen. Not like a wolf at all. She was something else. Something full of magic.

And Mama was trapped inside the magic.

11. THE WITCH

Early the next morning, when the sun had barely lit the land, Pa pounded on my door. I was already dressed and ready.

"Where will we go?" I asked. He handed me my rifle. It was loaded. "Are we going to kill the brown wolf?"

"If you see it, kill it."

I waited for him to tell me more, but he did not. We left and went straight for the wood. Pa carried some supplies on his back and stomped through the thick brush ahead of me.

I had seen my father like this at other times. When the winter was setting in, or when the scorching sun threatened the crops. In those times, he barely ate, or spoke, or slept. Then the scare would pass. His empty eyes would come back to life. Pa would re-emerge.

We walked for what felt like hours. My rifle grew heavier with every step. Pa stormed through the wood letting branches swing back without a thought. I learned to leave a little distance between us, but I had to walk fast to keep up. I kept my head down and used my ears. Pa's heavy footsteps tore into the untouched forest bed layered with forest matter. Unexpected dips and notches in the terrain jarred my ankles. The twists and turns were endless. Pa seemed to charge as deeply into the recesses of the forest as possible.

Finally, when the sun burned high above the treetops and I was sweating and aching for a rest, he stopped walking. I bent over gasping.

After a moment, I realized Pa was standing still. I peered around him half expecting to see Mama again, the wolf Mama.

Instead, we had arrived at a desolate cabin. It was small and made with moss-covered logs barely stripped, and fitted together crudely. Vines encased it like the weaved cocoon of a spider's prey. A crooked chimney crushed into it on one side. There was no place swept in front of the door. Haphazard patches of herbs and strange ivies grew around the perimeter.

My stomach knotted. Who, or what, lived shut up in a house like this so deep into the wood? But I knew. Only witches lived deep in the wood.

"Pa?"

"Quiet."

He motioned for me to follow him.

To my distress, we approached the door. I pressed into him from behind, clutching the rifle tight in my trembling hands.

He knocked. It was a soft sound muffled by the moss. I hoped whatever lived inside didn't hear it.

After a long moment, the door unlatched. It creaked open a few inches shaking sprinkles of earth matter onto us from the vegetation above. The vine seemed to prevent the door from opening more, hardly yielding to the push from inside.

Pa repositioned himself to look in, to look at the thing that had answered. I moved with him, stuck fast against him, my face buried in his back. I could only imagine what it was.

"I need your help." Pa's voice lacked its usual strength. Nothing answered. "It's my wife," he said. "She was bitten. She has been a wolf since last night. Gone somewhere into this wood." Still nothing. "Please, I beg you."

The terrible truth hit me. We were not looking for Mama. Not yet. This rotting house had been our destination all along. We were seeking help from a diabolical means deep in the dark parts of the forest. Not a doctor, or the sheriff, or even other townsfolk. And Pa had said Mama was bitten. He spoke as though he knew all along about such things.

"Come," said a high, tottering and ancient voice.

Pa took hold of the door in his big hand and pulled it against the strain of the vine. Stale air escaped the dark dwelling with hints of a smell like burning grass. I clung to Pa's shirt to hold him back, but he moved forward, dragging me into the musty dimness with him.

I could hear a thump and long scratching sound, like a body being dropped and dragged. I dared to peek.

A lumpy form hobbled along, leading us inside. It was draped with a cloak of rags that seemed made of the same material as the butcher's apron and with the same dark stains. It limped ahead with one foot trailing behind until it came to the hearth and was illuminated by some firelight. It poked dwindling flames with a long stick and then waved that behind at us. "Sit down," it said. I looked over at a small table with two wooden chairs. I wondered who usually sat in the other one.

Pa didn't move.

Then to my horror, it said, "Peel that child from your hips and let's have a look at him."

I gasped and clutched Pa, but he wretched me off and pushed me away so I stood in front of him wide-eyed and stricken.

The thing turned. It had matted, old hair laden with bits of the forest. The face was made of pale eyes, a pointed chin and the wrinkled, sucking kind of lips that go with toothless mouths. Round-balled cheeks protruded below its eyes like a haunted doll. Skin hung from its bones. It was a lady, in a way. A witch. She wanted to eat me, I knew.

"Pretty boy. Small for his age, yes?" She looked me up and down. Warm terror turned my limbs to wax.

"He manages," Pa replied.

"Fair skin. Hair of gold. Pretty boy."

For the first time, I noticed how different I looked from my ruddy father. The witch was right. My skin never browned as much as Pa's. It kept its whiteness, like Mama's.

The witch sighed and began shuffling along again. I watched her make her way around the table to a corner of the hovel that seemed to be the kitchen. Makeshift shelving was filled with corked, glass bottles. Each contained various amounts of colored liquids or objects. I scanned them for people parts. Nothing appeared to have been taken from humans, until my eyes fell on the skull. It sat among the vials with its hollow holes gazing in our direction and the jawbone missing. I looked away and pretended I hadn't seen it, in case the witch would realize her plans to eat me were found out and she acted upon them directly.

"You should have come sooner," she said, rummaging through the liquids, bottles clanking. "It will be difficult now."

Pa hung his head. "The fault is mine. I did not believe it."

I looked up at him in surprise. Understanding began to stab up my chest. Pa and Mama had known something was wrong, but Pa never believed the old stories. If Pa and Mama had come to the witch before last night, perhaps all would be well.

For a moment, I felt angry. But Pa's shoulders slumped as he scrutinized the dark floor. Pa would have never let anything happen to Mama on purpose. It was alarming to see him like this.

"Werewolves are not new to these parts," the witch was saying. "They were gone for many years. They have returned."

"What will happen to her?"

The witch shook a bottle and looked at its bubbling contents.

"She is a wolf. She will be a wolf. Kill like a wolf. Eat like a wolf. Sleep where a wolf sleeps. Go where a wolf goes."

Pa voiced my thoughts. "Will she return to her human form at the end of the full moon, like the legends say?"

The witch shook her head. "Legends tell of a creature that is more human that wolf. It is not so. A werewolf is more wolf than human. She will not return."

Pa pinched the bridge of his nose with his fingers. "If a werewolf is a wolf, why were we attacked?"

"Did the werewolf attack *you*?" The witch sneered. "He bit your wife, yes?"

"Yes, but-"

"Not you. Not your boy. Yes?"

"Yes," he said slowly. "He?"

"It must have been a 'he' then, yes?"

Pa stared at her. When he said nothing, the witch looked up.

"Wolves are not solitary creatures," she said. "They desire family and are lonely without it. Winter is here. Come spring, there'll be pups." Now she gave an awful smile. "It's nearly mating time. Pretty boy. Pretty *wife*."

Pa's voice came out thick. "That won't happen. I'll find her. What do I have to do."

"It will be difficult now," she repeated in a sing-song way.

The witch had a bottle in her hand that she liked now. She ambled back to us. I backed away.

"Sap of wolfbane flower," she said. "There is plenty enough. It kills a wolf but not a werewolf. It will only reverse the spell on a werewolf. If your wife consumes this, the curse will be broken. Beware, for it is deadly poison. Don't let it touch you."

The liquid sloshed in her shaking grip until Pa took the bottle and concealed it in his shirt. "How will she drink it?"

The witch cackled. "It will be difficult now," she sang. "You should have come sooner."

"Where will I find her?"

"Ha! See many wolves, do you?"

Pa glared at her. He had always told me wolves were rarely seen. They flee from humans.

"If you are lucky, she mayn't be far. Perhaps she will yet recognize you and let you approach. You should make haste."

Pa turned to go at once, but the witch stamped her stick on the floor. "And what will you give an old woman in return? Just a poor, old woman, I am." Her eyes flew to me.

Pa put his arm in front of me. I cowered behind it.

"What do I do with a boy?" the witch scoffed. "Though what could I not do with a snip of golden hair? Such a pretty boy." Her voice rang higher as she considered the top of my head.

"Nothing from my son."

She scowled. "Fine. This time, I will have the food in your satchel."

"Of course," Pa said. "I thank you."

He emptied the contents of his pack on her table. We left her in there picking through the food with her skeleton fingers. I clung to Pa even as he tramped wildly along. I did not let go of his clothing until the cabin had completely disappeared behind us.

The walk back through the wood was much faster this time. We burst into our yard before I knew it. My legs throbbed. My hands and face burned with scratches.

"We will eat," Pa said, sounding strange being the one to announce supper. "Then, we get ready for tomorrow. We'll leave at first light."

"What about the farm?"

"Jim will care for it."

I wondered what Uncle Jim would think of Pa's request. Or rather, to Pa's *reason* for his request.

That night, I did as I was told. I packed my warmest clothing. The snow would soon fly. I knew it from the look of the sky and the feel of the air. The birds were scarce. We were no longer on the cusp of winter. We had taken the first step into it.

111. THE WINTER

We set out as soon as it was light enough to see through the trees. I wondered what Pa had said to Uncle Jim. Pa had a tent, blankets, oil and the lamp, and other supplies heaped upon his back. I carried our clothing.

We went north, a different direction from the witch's cabin, I noted in relief. And we walked slower than before with the extra weight. Every once in a while, Pa stopped to listen. We would stand still, hearing all the sounds around us. Pa studied marks in the earth, tree bark and feces.

All along, I envisioned the brown werewolf with his uncaring eyes. I thought of him taking my sweet Mama into some far, desolate place and thwarting her attempts to escape. Pa probably did, too.

When the sun set, I began to shiver. Pa found a small clearing to make camp. The most welcome sound of the day was the snapping of flames eating kindling. As the fire danced to life, its warmth spread over us. I hated moving away from the blaze into our tent, but I burrowed deep into my blanket until my own body heat filled the space. Even though we were in the middle of the wood where demons must surely lurk, I was too tired now to care.

In the morning, we gobbled down our breakfast, packed, and set out again. Pa continued to lead in the same direction, listening to the wood as he went.

Days began to pass this way. We shared few words because Pa wanted to listen. He told me only that he had known of wolves living in these parts. It was a good place to start.

Soon enough, we woke one morning to freshly fallen snow. I could see my breath in the air. I put on extra woolen socks and tucked my trousers into my boots like Pa.

The ground had hardened under the snow making it easier to traipse through the wood but not so easy to see where I was going. Once, I slipped and thought I injured my ankle. Pa glowered at me.

"Get up, boy," he said.

I limped for a while as the pain worked its way out. Pa seemed relieved that we did not have the inconvenience of an injury. He took my rifle from me then, freeing my hands.

"Be more careful," he said.

"Yes, Pa."

The deeper into the mountains we went, the more the snow fell. Icy treetops glistened above and the earth floor reflected the light for as far as we could see. All was still. We rarely heard a new sound. It was easier to see prints in the snow though. Pa liked that. It was just harder to start a fire.

At last, one morning, we came upon a carcass. This was clearly good news. The tension in Pa's face eased for the first time.

"Do you know what this is?"

"A deer," I said, observing the size of the ribcage, clean of its meat and frosted over. Tracks were everywhere. Bear tracks, fox, even bird, little feet I did not recognize, and, miracle of miracles, wolf, too.

"This is a wolf's kill. The animals share the food once the wolves are finished," he explained.

We made camp near the bones. Not long after, we came upon other remains. These were also picked clean, and fresher.

That night, as Pa roasted bits of squirrel meat, the sound we had been waiting for came floating through the air. It was a long, sorrowful howl.

My eyes met Pa's. He tilted his head back to listen, the corners of his lips turning up. Everything else in the forest fell silent. The howl was followed by another, and then another. The chorus echoed into the night. Mournful cries harmonizing together. It continued on for several minutes and then died out.

"We're close," Pa said. Then his eyes darkened, his little bit of happiness stamped out. "But if she's here, she's with them. She's not alone."

The next morning, as we were packing up camp, I saw movement in the corner of my eye. I froze. At first, it was camouflaged by the forest. Then a face emerged. Two pointed ears upon a gray mask that tapered into a long muzzle. A wolf was watching us.

Pa was next to me in an instant. We stared at the wolf and the wolf stared at us for what felt like a long time. It was not Mama. And it was not the brown wolf. It was gray with white on its face and chest. It did not look angry. Just wary. Finally, it weaved silently through the trees. It ran parallel to our campsite keeping its eyes on us. Then behind it, another appeared, following in the path of the first. This one was smaller but with the same markings. Then another. Black. Two more, even smaller, reddish brown and white. Followed lastly by my mother.

I opened my mouth, but Pa clamped his giant hand over my face. He pushed so hard that my nose stung. The wolf pack ignored us as they trotted through the wood and disappeared. I was still looking after them when Pa released me to knock my head with his hand. My ears rung.

"What're you thinking?" he hissed.

"I'm sorry, Pa." I held my tingling head in my hands.

"They've trusted us now, see? Don't scare them off."

"Yes, Pa."

"Hurry, we'll follow them."

I had never seen a wolf before except the scarred werewolf. These looked like dogs. I didn't know if I could shoot a dog.

Thankfully, we soon saw that Pa was right. The wolves were getting used to us and were not going to hide from us now. They even started to play in our sight. It first happened many yards away. The smaller ones yipped and whined and pounced until the others engaged in romping around. It was strange to watch the white wolf play. She did not seem like she could be Mama. It was only a wolf that frolicked around, bowing playfully, tail wagging. Not her. Perhaps we were mistaken about the whole thing. Maybe we were mad after all. Maybe something else had happened to Mama.

As the days passed, I became mesmerized with them. The pack would look to the largest wolf and know what he was telling them. He led them into hunts and away from danger. He was the one to begin the long, celebratory howling after a meal. He loved them, and most of all, he loved my mother.

Mama and the big wolf rarely passed each other without brushing shoulders or exchanging a lick. I started to notice this at the same time as Pa. I was grateful the big wolf protected her, but it made Pa's breathing shudder. His nostrils would flare as he watched them together. He glared at that poor wolf and sometimes even looked like he was going to raise his rifle.

One afternoon, the two smaller wolves appeared in a small, soft meadow not far from our camp. The trees were thinning in these parts as we climbed higher into the mountains. The animals playfully tugged on one another's ears, and when they spotted me, their tails wagged. Their eyes were bright and expectant.

"Go on," Pa said, sending me to build deeper trust with the pack.

I slowly walked toward them through the freshly fallen snow of the clearing. They let me approach. They sniffed the air as I came and then my outstretched hands. Their teeth were longer and sharper than a dog, but they had the same kind eyes. Their tails wagged. One bowed and barked. I bent to touch it. It hit my hand with its nose and ran in a circle, luring me into playtime like a puppy. I began to run around the little meadow with the young wolves. Until they stopped.

Suddenly, I saw that the gray and white leader stood erect a mere ten feet from us. He had emerged from the trees on the other side of the meadow. The tails of the youngsters went under their legs. Their ears peeled back as they slinked away from me in the big wolf's direction. His mouth opened into a small snarl for me, but something told me he was not angry, just worried.

I didn't know what to do. I did the first thing I could think. I bowed to him and stayed down on the ground the way I had seen the other wolves do. I heard him creep to me. I felt him sniff my hair. Then in a flash, he and the others were gone.

When I stood, I glanced over my shoulder and saw that Pa had his rifle aimed right at me. I should have known he would have a reason to shoot the big wolf if it came near me. I ran back to Pa, but he didn't put the weapon down.

"Pa," I said breathlessly. "He's good, Pa. He's not a werewolf. You don't have to kill him. It's all going right." I put my hand on his shoulder. He flinched. Finally, when he looked at me, he lowered the rifle.

"They're all males," he muttered.

All except my mother. For whatever reason, she was not held prisoner by the brown werewolf, but another wolf had taken possession of her.

The next morning, I awoke to a shot. I raced out of the tent into the meadow. Pa was trudging through the tall mounds of snow with his rifle resting across his shoulder. Grief gripped me. I thought I might vomit. I didn't want to know, but I had to. I ran through the clearing and rushed ahead of him. Tears already stung my cheeks.

"It's not the wolf, boy," I heard him say. In my blurring vision, I saw hoofs protruding from a snow pile. I pushed the tops of frosted, dead grass out of my way and gazed down at the dead deer. Relief washed over me.

He had shot a deer. Why? Pa was never wasteful. We had nothing to keep the meat.

Pa came up behind me. "You'd think you loved them more than your own mother."

It had been weeks since we'd left home. We were dirty, miserable and sick at heart. We were always wet and cold, and we had long been out of the food we had packed. Small animals and fish supplied us with meals, but they were scarce.

As a boy, I did not comprehend the danger of running out of food or how difficult it was to find it every day. Pa made it seem easy, and I trusted him with my child's faith. Only looking back now do I grasp the anxiety he must have felt. Pa's barking orders became the only communication between us. He didn't even seem to like me anymore. All I knew was that if we didn't get Mama back, I would probably lose them both for good.

Pa sliced open the doe's belly with his hunting knife. Blood and entrails leaked into the snow. "It's for your wolves," he said scornfully and walked away. He did not even take any meat for us. I followed him back across the meadow.

After what felt like a long time, the wolf leader appeared to investigate Pa's kill. A peace offering, was it? But I knew Pa looked too menacing for that as he observed the leader sniffing the meat. Soon, the wolf let out a howl. It was a call to the others. They came out of the wood one by one and helped devour the deer.

Pa smiled a dark, satisfied smile.

In the next few days, Pa spent his time hunting. He managed small game for us, but he was obsessed with finding another deer for the wolves. I wanted to ask him why, but I felt afraid. Most often, he did not want me to talk anyway. He just wanted me to be quiet while he hunted or watched the wolves.

Eventually, a few small doe wandered into the meadow. When I saw them, I covered my ears. Within moments, a shot rang out. We rushed to the fallen victim. The other deer vanished.

When we came upon the writhing animal, Pa had to shoot it again. I hated when that happened. Pa leaned down and opened the belly of this one, too, but this time, he rolled back on his heels and took something from his coat.

At once, I understood. Pa uncorked the bottle of the witch's drink with his knife.

"But Pa."

"Shush, Jesse."

His eyes blazed. There was no stopping him, but I had to try.

"It will kill the others," I said meekly.

"It might."

My thoughts raced. "It might kill Mama, too. How do you know?"

He looked at me then. "Your mother is already gone. If it doesn't work, she's still gone." And then, "I'm sorry, Jesse. I can't help it about the others."

As he poured the liquid into the opening of the deer, tears filled my eyes. When he corked the empty bottle, stood and walked away, a sob escaped me. Pa's big hand came crashing down as I knew it would, covering my face. He snatched me up and shook me.

"Stop that," he said. He actually carried me back to our viewing place but not to be kind. I was making too much of a racket with my crying.

The wolves trusted us now. They trusted me. How could we do this to them? Murder their whole family? Even the young ones? The wolves never killed ruthlessly. They killed to survive, and they shared their food with the whole forest. Now they would all be dead. The scavengers would come and pick at their bones instead. I couldn't stand the thought. What would Mama think? Would she hate us? Did she love them?

"Shut up," Pa hissed. He sat down to watch. After some time, two gray ears appeared above a snow drift. The leader looked around sniffing the air, watching our direction, maybe even seeing us. He approached the crumpled form of the deer. He sniffed and gave it a tentative lick. He turned his head slightly as though he might walk away. Maybe he could smell the poison? But just as I dared to hope he would leave, his head tilted back, and he howled.

It was a call to come and die. He did not know it. The other wolves began to run from the wood. Beside me, Pa watched the sight with bloodshot, red-rimmed eyes. His lips formed a more threatening grimace than the wolves'.

I couldn't watch. I tried to look away, but it wasn't enough. A pain welled up within my chest so big I thought I would burst. Adrenaline surged through my body, ringing in my ears, heating every nerve. I couldn't let this happen.

Before I knew what I was doing, I found myself charging into the meadow. Pa tried to snatch me, but I eluded his grasp. The sound of my screaming pierced the air.

"No! Get away from it! No! No!"

I screamed all the way to the deer. When I reached it, my eyes met those of the gray leader. My instincts had betrayed me. His teeth were bared and his body ready to pounce. The other wolves snarled and gathered behind him, waiting for him to lunge into an attack. Too late I remembered that dogs protected their food. Too late I remembered these wolves protected one another.

I dropped to the ground as I had done before. The snarling only increased. It came closer. The gray wolf was going to die anyway now. Pa would shoot him any second. Or I would die. I hoped I wouldn't stay alive long while the wolf was tearing me apart.

Suddenly, there were soft footfalls beside me, and the snarling quieted. I lifted my head to see the paws of the white wolf. Mama stood between me and the pack leader.

I tilted my neck to look up at her face. She stood tall and gazed daringly at the pack leader. He growled and seemed to demand she back down, but she would not. Finally, he relaxed his stance, snorted and turned back to the deer.

Mama growled low and deep. The leader's eyes darted back to her in surprise. Again he lowered to take a bite, but Mama snapped at him. He cocked his head to the side, looked at me and back up at her. He whined a little. In the end, he decided to walk away, taking the others with him.

Mama nudged me with her head and bent to lick my cheek, still wet with tears.

"Mama," I said. "You have to eat it. It won't hurt *you*. Please, Mama. It's magic."

When she did not move or seem to understand, I crawled to

the carcass. Mama followed. I pointed at it, but she only watched me. I reached my hand into the pile of entrails intending to take a piece. It wasn't easy. I managed only to pull off a tiny shred of something. I held my palm out to the wolf. Her eyes looked very much like Mama's then. She gently took the bloody nibble from my hand, licked her lips, and then sank her teeth into the belly of the deer. She ate as daintily as a wolf could.

After a moment, I heard a gurgling sound from deep within her. She hunched as if in pain and darted away into the snow drifts.

"Fee!"

Pa came from behind me charging after her. We ran, following her prints into the wood. Just ahead, at the edge of a narrow icy creek, my human mother lay crumpled in the snow.

We bounded to her and fell down beside her, calling her name. She was naked and cradling her stomach. Her tangled, dark hair sprawled out in the white snowbank.

"Mama! Wake up!" I said.

But Pa had stopped moving. He was staring down at her with a horrified expression. I followed his gaze to Mama's stomach. It swelled largely. I wondered for a moment if it was the poison. Then in a sickening instant, I knew. I had seen a woman with child before.

My eyes migrated slowly back to Pa. He was rigid and gaping at her. If I had any doubt that Mama had not been expecting a child before her disappearance, it went away at the sight of him.

As if to bring us from our thoughts, she made a small, whimpering sound.

"Mama," I said, nudging her. "It's me, Jesse."

She opened her eyes to slits as though the sun blinded her. She moved her lips, but no sound came out.

I put my arms around her. "She's freezing, Pa."

This seemed to finally jolt him. He took off his coat and wrapped Mama inside it. She wondered up at him as he lifted her into his arms. Then her head rested against him, and she was asleep.

I didn't want to be away from Mama, but I knew I could not leave the deer. Pa had already started back to camp, so I slinked away. He would not want me destroying the poison. He would want the gray wolf dead now more than ever. But he did not even notice me leave.

When I arrived back at camp after burning the deer, Mama was still asleep. Pa sat by a fire, still as a stone. Both loaded rifles leaned against a tree within his easy reach.

Just as I started to wonder what the wolf pack must be thinking, a painful howling sliced into the night. It sounded different than before. They grieved Mama. I didn't blame them. Just then, a low, yowling sound came from inside the tent to join them. Pa must have heard her, too, but he pretended he didn't.

I thought having Mama back would be the end of our ordeal. But I knew now it was the beginning of something else. Pa was not any better. He was much worse.

IV. THE WATCHING

The next day, nothing changed with Mama. Our journey was difficult. For one, Mama was disoriented and agitated. She seemed frightened of clothing and fire and only vaguely recognized us. In addition, she did not speak. She made grunts and whimpers in response to our talking. She was disinterested in us and only eyed us cautiously when we came near. We had to hold her arms and guide her along or she would wander off or stop to investigate a smell or a sound.

Of course, the most difficult of all was her condition. She sometimes grabbed at her big belly and let out little cries. I was terrified when she did this, and Pa's shoulders crunched up high. Neither of us said it, but we both wondered what was growing inside her. Could my mother give birth to wolf pups and survive? We had to get her to the doctor. I thought it was the plan, but Pa did not seem to be in such a rush now. When he looked at Mama, I could only read one feeling. Betrayal.

Each night, the long howls erupted, but they became more distant. I was glad the wolves had not followed us, but I missed them. I often wondered what it would be like to join them. They were happy, innocent and free. I was starting to understand how Mama must feel.

When we finally arrived at the farm, it felt like a dream. Even if Mama could not be grateful for milk and eggs, soft beds, or even the roof over her head, Pa and I relished the comforts.

After we had eaten and rested, Pa said, "I'm going to Jim's. I'll tell him…what I need to."

I could not imagine taking one more step. I didn't even mind being left with Mama on my own as long as I didn't have to go anywhere else.

"No one can know about your mother," Pa said before walking out the door.

I admitted he was probably right. People would be afraid of her. *More wolf than human*, the witch had said. But would she survive what was about to happen to her without help?

A mere four weeks later, it was Mama's time. It was spring, just as the witch had predicted. Mama had resigned herself to life in the farmhouse being watched over closely by Pa and I and helped to do just about everything. Just as she had done before she disappeared, Mama sat every night in her chair facing the window and looking listlessly into the sky. Another full moon came and went, but Mama stayed Mama. She still had not spoken a word.

The afternoon it happened, Mama clutched her stomach and dropped to the floor. She cried out. The bulge had grown so much in the time since we brought her back that I wondered how her skin did not tear. She seemed to be in pain all the time, but today was much worse. I pulled her up and supported her weight as best as I could to walk her to her bedroom.

"All will be well, Mama. I'll get Pa."

I want to say the delivery was quick and easy, but really I would have rather gone back into the woods with Pa for another few months than to take part in it. Everything about it horrified me. Pa barked orders over Mama's wails. Then finally, when Pa could see some part of what came out of her, a familiar look flashed in his eyes.

Panic gripped me. He couldn't. Mama screamed louder. What would I do if he tried to kill it, whatever it was? I would not be able to stop him this time.

But with one final effort from Mama, Pa caught something small in his hands, and a human baby's cry escaped it. I closed my eyes and exhaled.

Pa looked at the slimy thing with mild disgust but slowly wrapped it in a blanket and deposited it into my mother's waiting arms. All I could see of it was thick, reddish hair that was matted with goo. It was hard to believe something so small had seemed so big.

"A girl," Pa said to me.

Mama looked down at the babe. Her eyes flashed. The wildness seemed to vanish from them. To our shock, her lips parted, and she said, "Red."

Sweating and haggard, Pa kneeled by the bedside. My mother turned her gaze to him for the first time. Her pretty eyes met his. She reached out a hand to caress his cheek.

She said, "Abe."

And just like magic, Pa forgave her, and my baby sister, and maybe even the gray wolf.

V. The Wolf Child

It didn't take Mama long to come back to herself after Red's birth. It took Pa longer, but he had always been a hard man. I had thought whatever was inside Mama might make things even worse, but the baby somehow made both of my parents turn human anew. It was just the way of her.

Red had a natural magic that put us all at ease. Her bright eyes and gentle smile captivated us. She watched everything we did and determined to follow exactly, learning quickly and almost never having to be scolded. She spilled deep wonder into our souls so that we were never melancholy anymore. We started to forget that we ever had been. Light even twinkled in Pa's eyes. He began to clasp me on the back as if in a little hug. The tiny show of affection meant the world to me. And Red was to thank for it.

Red's wolf side showed itself though. Just as she had been born quickly, she grew quickly. It took her half the amount of time as a normal child to reach the same milestones. She was never knocked off balance and was never injured. She just floated through our world like a dream casting away our momentary troubles and engaging us in playfulness, just as the wolf pack had done for me when I watched them from afar.

When her yellow-gold eyes met ours, we always knew what she was thinking. She held cheerful conversations with us, encouraging us, joking, and laughing often. She had a delighted laugh that bubbled up from inside and exploded into clean, contagious giggles. She would throw her head back for this, flashing pointed, white teeth inside delicate, red lips.

Nine years passed as quickly as the blooming of a flower. We could not tell anyone where Red had come from, so we said we found her in the wood. A search was done, but when no parents turned up, Pa and Mama were given permission to become her legal guardians. We kept Red hidden away on the farm rarely letting anyone visit. We stopped going into town as often and almost never took Red with us when we did. It would be too obvious to others that she was different.

Mama had resorted to educating us both at home so it was not strange that I went to school but not Red. I liked that much better anyway, and I was able to spend more time with Pa. The hurt of his previous indifference had all but faded away.

It was Mama who first surmised that Red would not live as long as the rest of us. It made sense. At nine years old, the girl seemed to be closer to my age, if not older. Her thick, red tresses reached far below her shapely waist. She was a lady any man would admire.

One day in mid-autumn, I was taking Red for a walk in the forest behind the house. We knew why she loved the outdoors, but we always felt uneasy about it. Something inside us seemed to warn that if Red had enough of a taste of the wild, she may not want to stay with us. When we objected to her solitary strolls, she would put her head down as if in submission. That was why she often secretly begged me to take her, and I usually consented. I remembered the joyful play of the free wolves, and I knew we were keeping something sacred from her.

I was always careful, though. I never walked with her to the south, where Pa and I had gone to find the witch's cabin. And I never went to the north toward the territory of the wolves. We traveled east always.

The wood stilled that day like always. Wild animals vanished when Red was near. We had not even seen a deer wander by the apple tree in all the years since she had been born.

My sister was wearing a white and yellow checkered dress with a full apron. As we walked, she plucked wildflowers and leaves, pieces of bark and even twigs. She sniffed and tasted some of these and collected her treasurers in her apron. While Pa and I tended to the farm, Red would explore the natural world around her. She prepared healing remedies, scents for the house and soap, and she was in charge of the herb garden for cooking.

"What will you do when you're grown?" she asked me. Sunbeams stroked her cheek.

"What do you mean?"

"You know. You only have a few more years of school. Will you always stay and help Pa, or will you travel to other places? Like you did before I came?"

"I was a boy. We never went far." That life seemed so long ago.

"Still you got to go to town every week," she said. "Sometimes more than that. I never get to go."

"The town's not safe for you." I repeated the words we always said to her.

"I know. It's safe for *you* though. You could go anywhere if you wanted. Don't you ever feel like you want to?" She stepped into a patch of sunlight. It danced on her skin as the leaves rustled overhead. She inhaled, closing her eyes and letting the heat of the light soak into her. She looked like she belonged there amid the changing leaves and old trees.

She suddenly opened her eyes. "What?"

I had been thinking that she would make a good wife for someone one day if it were only safe to let that happen. We had decided that since Red aged so quickly, it was best that she stay with us until the end. We would take care of her and enjoy every moment of our time together. Of course, that also meant it would be hard for me to find a wife for myself one day, but it was my choice to help protect Red. How could I not? It was all my family had done from the time she entered our lives. It had bonded us together again. We were never been happier.

I smiled. "Nothing. And no, Red. I like it here with Mama, and Pa, and you. You didn't know Pa before."

Her small brow furrowed.

"He was always a good man," I said. "He just did not always openly love us. He does that now. I used to think about leaving, but now I just want to stay and take care of all of you, like Pa does."

She gave me a chastising look with gentle eyes. "You're the best brother I could ask for, but you worry about me too much."

"Someone's got to."

She giggled. "Everyone does!"

I gave her shoulder a light squeeze. "I know you would do just fine on your own."

"Why can't I walk on my own then?"

"Why would you want to?"

She shook her head. "I wonder if all big brothers are this way?"

"Probably."

"Well, when *I'm* grown, I will travel far from here."

I had known Red longed to explore the wood, but I had never heard her voice this desire before. She looked dreamily ahead, a smile on her lips, hair swaying with each step. We had never told her our thoughts about her future, and we never would.

"Where do you want to go?" I asked.

"For one, I want to see what's in this forest that you don't want me to know about."

"I don't know what you mean."

"Don't be silly. I know you take me on all the same paths." When I didn't answer, she grinned. "It's alright. I like the mystery."

We limited her so much, but she always forgave us.

"Wait," she said suddenly, throwing out an arm to stop me.

"What is it?"

"Shh." She strained her ears and squinted her eyes. I looked but saw nothing. Red always heard and saw things I didn't.

"There," she said under her breath and pointed ahead. I followed her finger and saw it. My blood froze. I did not want to believe it was the brown werewolf from years ago, but his ghastly scar gave him away. My thoughts raced. I didn't have a rifle. I had stopped bringing one along years ago. No animals ever came near us with Red around. I should have remembered the fearlessness of the Were. Under no circumstances could either of us be bitten. If it did attack us, it would have to be me. I would fight it to the death.

"Back away slowly," I said.

Red looked at the animal with a curious expression. She wasn't afraid, of course.

"Red, that's the werewolf that bit Mama." She didn't seem to hear me. "Red."

At last she began to obey. "That's really him?" she asked.

We backed away, and the Were stayed. I hurried her through the wood watching behind me all the way. "Tell me if you hear him," I demanded. For a moment, I felt like Pa. I looked down at my hands that gripped my sister's arms. They were so big compared to her. I released her. There was never a need to be forceful with Red. She always did as she was told.

"I'm sorry," I said. "That wolf attacked Mama, and I don't want it to hurt you."

"*Did* he attack her?" she asked, almost to herself as we rushed along.

"He bit her. It may have been worse if Pa hadn't been there."

"And that made her a wolf?" Her words were airy, as if she were piecing the story together for the first time. We had told her many times.

I no longer feared the werewolf the way I feared Red's response to him. She had looked at him the way I once looked at the wolf pack years ago. They did not mean any harm. That's all I had ever wanted Pa to believe. He refused to see them the way I did. His priority was saving Mama. My priority was saving Red.

"Yes. A werewolf. It's how we got you. And we wouldn't change it for the world, but it's not something any of us wants to do over again."

She didn't say anything else. I led her back through the wood and safely home. There would be no more walks. In fact, Red wouldn't even go outside.

After supper, I sat with Pa at the table loading all of our rifles.

"You sure it was him?"

"He had the scar."

"Why is he not dead?" Anger simmered his words. "It's been nine whole years."

None of the werewolf legends spoke of immortality, but I wondered if we might be wrong about Red's aging. If the werewolf was still alive and doing well, maybe that magic had gone into

Red? We had no one to compare her with.

I looked over at the sitting area. Mama and Red were together, their backs to us, facing the picture window. Neither of them had said much during supper, but both listened to our orders. *Don't go outside. Tell us if you see anything. Tell us if you hear anything.* They listened to our brooding and our planning, and they watched us pace and fret. I had not noticed them slip into that old, melancholy silence. It was the first time I had seen it since Mama emerged from it so long ago.

The brown werewolf always did this to us. One visit by him always changed our whole world. I hated him.

The next few days were a blur. Pa and I kept our rifles with us while we worked. With winter approaching, there was a lot to do. We left Mama and Red in the house each day, blinds drawn, doors locked. We saw their sadness but ignored it. They would forgive us later. For now, it had to be this way.

Pa and I occasionally scouted the surrounding wood for tracks. It seemed we might be clear of the werewolf. He could have just been passing through. Though we could never be too sure. Memories of our endless journey played in both of our minds. The witch. The snow and cold. The days of scarce food and no sign of hope. Nearly destroyed relationships. The secrets. The hiding.

No. I had Mama, Pa and Red now. I was not willing to lose any of them.

Pa and I stood posted on the front porch one night sharing a bottle of whiskey. We did not often do it, but tonight we were finally starting to relax. It had been seven days. No wolf sightings. No howls. Nothing.

"You think we're safe?" I asked.

He gazed into the shadows of the yard. "I think so. Your mother needs fresh air or is liable to wilt away. Poor Red does not speak to me. You?"

I shook my head. "Her fearlessness scares me. I don't want her to be afraid, but I don't want her to be so trusting, either."

Pa took a long swig of drink. He sighed. "That's the struggle of a man. When to protect. When to let go."

I glanced over at him, surprised. His face was hidden in the dark, but I could make out the form of him leaning against the post. I didn't need to see him. I knew what he looked like standing there in his overalls identical to mine. I'd watched him my entire life. And I'd become like him. For better or worse, I had.

"What should we do?" I asked.

He laughed dryly. "I've never been good at this."

It was an apology. Though I knew now I probably would not have done things any differently myself.

"I imagine when they start to look like they do, it's probably time to let go," he said.

If I had not been so preoccupied with watching for the werewolf, I might have noticed that the moon was nearly full.

The next morning, we told Mama and Red they could go outside.

"*Finally,*" Red said.

Mama frowned at us as she brushed passed. As soon as the sun hit her, she seemed to revive. She had been preparing the flower gardens for winter when we banned her from the yard. Red followed her. I wanted to stay with them.

"Jesse," Pa said. "Let's go."

I gave them a final look as they strolled away.

That evening was especially good. Both Mama and Red laughed through supper, rehashing memories, telling stories. They were back to themselves and even happier than usual.

Red and I cleaned the dishes after.

"I love you, you know," she said, taking a wet plate from me to dry.

"I know. I'm sorry we treated you like that. We were just scared, that's all."

"You don't have to be sorry." She looked up at me, eyes shining, smiling. "I know why you did it. You're a good brother. You're going to make a good father one day, too."

She had never said anything like that to me before. Here she was talking about the future again. If being a father was in any way as stressful as protecting her, I wasn't sure how true her statement could be. Though a part of me hoped she was right. The hidden part of me that once in a while thought about having my own family thanked her for the encouragement, even if I doubted myself.

Red, who never doubted herself, said, "And I'm going to make a good mother. You don't have to say it. I know." She giggled. I looked away so the pain wouldn't show.

"You've had the best example," I said.

"Yes." She sighed. "Mama just wants us both to be happy."

"Of course, she does."

"I want you to be happy, too."

I handed her another plate. "I am happy."

"You're a little bit happy. Promise me that you will make sure you are happy, no matter what?"

My hands stilled in the sudsy water. Did she know?

"Red, what are you…"

"Just promise." Her voice was urgent, but she appeared calm. She was like Mama that way.

What could I do? "Well, I promise."

"And you don't have to worry about me so much. You said yourself you know I'll be fine."

I gave her a sheepish look. I would never lock her up in the house again. Not now that I had seen how much it upset her.

110

Maybe Pa and I had overreacted.

"I know. I'll try," I said.

She put her arms around me and nuzzled her face into my ribs as she did.

We finished cleaning. Red migrated into the sitting room to cuddle next to Pa. I could hear their low voices in conversation. I imagined she had gentle words of forgiveness for him, too.

That night, I fell asleep easy, barely noticing the soft moonshine from the window that filled the small space. My bedroom had been small to start, but Pa had split it into two rooms so Red could have her own.

I woke sometime later to a wolf's howl outside. My eyes shot open. *Red. Mama.* Where were they?

I burst out of my bedroom and burst open my sister's door. Gone.

"Pa!" I shouted, racing down the stairs.

He was already running from his bedroom. "Where's Red?" he said at the same time I said, "Where's Mama?"

"In there," Pa said.

"Gone," I said.

We grabbed the loaded rifles by the door and rushed out into the darkness. We were so frenzied we didn't even see the wolf. Not right away.

"There!" Pa shouted, raising his rifle.

It stood placid at the forest base. Moonlight glinted off of its eyes. Soft eyes. The animal never flinched. A slowly stirring, dragging tail betrayed only peace. The wolf was red. All red.

"Pa, I said. "Don't shoot."

He was aimed to fire.

"Pa," I said, trying to keep my voice steady. "It's Red." His body went rigid. "It's Red," I repeated tightly. "Put it down."

Even as I spoke I almost didn't believe it, but the truth of my words caught up to us. The wolf was the most beautiful animal I had ever seen. Even more beautiful than the white wolf. Her fur was fuzzy and soft like a young pup's, not yet battered by the outdoors. Her body sleek and narrow. A dainty snout. She took a step forward. Golden, gleaming eyes.

"No," Pa breathed, lowering the weapon. "Why?"

Mama appeared between us. She crossed her arms and calmly watched the wolf, a small smile dancing across her lips.

I looked from her to Pa, who appeared ready to bolt the moment the wolf decided to run, and then to my sister. Her tail lifted and began to wag. She did a little bow and pawed the earth.

Mama curled her small hand around my bicep and squeezed. I imagined she held Pa's arm, too. The terrible truth seeped into my heart. Red meant to leave us. The after-supper conversation had been a goodbye.

My thoughts flew all around. How could this have happened? The werewolf must have bitten her. Had she hid a wound from us so easily? I thought back through the days since we had seen the werewolf lurking in the forest, but it was too late for those maddening thoughts now. It did not matter how it had happened. It had.

Hatred ricocheted through me bouncing off of each nerve. What did it want with us?

They desire family, the witch had said so long ago, *and are lonely without it.*

The brown werewolf had not looked at me at all, I suddenly realized. I had been too focused on Red's safety to pay attention. He had only looked at her. It was autumn again, just like it had been when he had come for Mama.

My sister's words echoed in my mind. *I'm going to make a good mother.*

She would be a wonderful mother, there was no doubt about it. If she only had the chance. The reality sunk into the pit of my stomach like a rock. She did not have a chance, except this one.

Red only half belonged to our world, but she could never belong to the wolves as a human. This way, she would finally have the things she wanted. She could explore the forest beyond my safely laid paths. She could go far into the world and see what most people never would. She could be a wife and a mother. Here with us, she would never have any of it.

Our love for Red had blinded Pa and I. We wanted her for ourselves. As always, she and Mama had been patient with us, loving us in spite of ourselves and submitting to our brazen, misguided version of love.

Red lifted her nose to the sky and let out a long, sorrowful howl.

It was time, but I wanted the moment to linger. I felt it slipping away like sand through my fingers. I couldn't grasp it.

Red gave us a final deep, knowing look. The sand ran out. She began to turn away.

"No!" Pa lunged forward but stopped as my mother tightened her grip. "Fee, I can't-" He broke into sobs, falling to the ground. The rifle thudded into the grass. "I can't-I can't." Mama knelt beside him, patting his back.

"All is well," she said. "You did good."

"No, no," he cried, shaking his head in his hands.

"Yes. You did good. Now you must let go."

He slumped into her arms.

She held him, looking over his head and giving an encouraging smile to Red. Without looking at me, Mama whispered, "Let go, Jesse."

No one could know more than Mama that Red would be safe and this was what she needed.

I stared at the back of Red's ears until she disappeared into the darkness. It was as though someone had died. I fell to my knees beside Mama and Pa and joined their embrace with tears streaming down my own face.

We never saw her again.

VI. THE WRITER

When I finished my schooling, I left for New York City. I studied botany and had many adventures cataloguing plants in unexplored areas. I saw myself as a modern alchemist joining the world of magic to the world of science. Academics did not believe in magic, but I had seen it. As time went on, I met my wife, and we raised two children. All of this was thanks to Red and my promise to her, which I did my best to honor.

Later, my wife and I returned to the farm to help care for Mama and Pa. After their passing, we stayed on. The busyness of life and the world's medley of people and noise had drowned out fierce memories of my sister.

Now, during the quiet nights on the farm when the moon is the only light, I imagine Red. I can see her eyes like puddles of gold. I can hear her laugh echoing.

The legend says that the wolf child returns to this region at full moon. As far as I know, my sister has never returned. I wonder if she is still alive. After all this time, I have never found a reason to believe immortality is possible by magic, but the scarred werewolf had looked exactly the same after nine years as he had in the barnyard when it all began. Instead of a life cut short in our world,

I hope Red has had a full, free life in the magic.

Before she left, Red taught us how to take and use the parts of the plants. I often wondered if it was only coincidence that I was drawn to study the natural world in her steps. For so many years now, just in case she ever comes home, I have always kept with me a jar of wolfbane sap.

Now you know why I must ask you to do the same in my stead. For Red.

First published in the Botanical Gazette, August, 1961.

MEG GRIMM

Meg Grimm is a Christian writer and researcher. She lives in Ohio-pyle, Pennsylvania with her husband Max and dog Bill. Her articles on biblical wisdom for natural health and beauty can be found at **CastleGardens.co.** Known as the Story Spinner, Meg's other books and folktale and fairy tale blog can be found at **StorySpinnerBooks. com.** Meg's avocations include soapmaking, herb gardening and independently studying folklore. Meg serves on the council at The Journey Church in Uniontown, where she helps coordinate various ministries.

FOLLOW MEG

Facebook	fb.me/meggrimmauthor
Twitter	@MegGrimmAuthor
Instagram	meggrimm.author
Parler	https://parler.com/profile/MegGrimm/posts
YouTube	Story Spinner Books; Finding Folklore

How to Become a Christian

The Bible teaches that all have sinned and deserve God's judgment. But God so loved the world that He sent His only Son Jesus, who lived a sinless life and died in our place. Jesus took our punishment instead! He resurrected from the dead three days later, defeating sin and death forever. If you believe this, repent of your sin and choose to trust Jesus, declaring that He is Lord and God. You will be saved from judgment and live eternally with Him in heaven. (John 1:12, 3:16.)

As a Christian (Christ follower), seek to become involved in a Bible-believing church fellowship. This is God's design for strengthening your own faith as well as blessing other believers, who are now your brothers and sisters in God's family. (Heb.10:24-25) Align yourself with Christian mentors who will help you understand all that took place at the moment of your salvation in Christ and who will walk with you on the next steps on this journey. Regularly read your Bible and pray to deepen in your personal relationship with Jesus. (Ps. 1:1-2, 1 Thess. 5:16-18)

Jesus loves you and has been waiting for you! He has a plan and purpose for your life, more than all you could ask for or imagine. (Eph. 3:14-21)

CPSIA information can be obtained
at www.ICGtesting.com
Printed in the USA
BVHW070449080922
646508BV00015B/381

9 781734 786767